Zephyr's Kiss

Tammy Teigland

Copyright 2013 © Tammy Teigland

Published August 14,2013

Prelude

Burlington, WI

Cal attentively gazed from across the kitchen table, resting his smoky-gray eyes on Kate.

The mischievous gleam in her green eyes fell upon Cal. As Kate took a sip of coffee, Cal felt her bare foot run up his leg and come to rest between his thighs.

Wide-eyed with surprise, she got his undivided attention. Flirtatiously eyeing Cal, Kate seductively bit her lower lip.

Cal raised an interested brow, "Did you want something?"

Kate gave Cal, her best sultry look in response.

"What's gotten into you this morning?"

"Just feeling...playful!"

He let out a long sigh, "What am I going to do with you?"

"If you need some suggestions, I can think of a few!"

With an impish grin, he rushed her, "So - can I!" He quickly wrapped his arms around her and playfully kissed and nibbled the back of her neck as she squealed.

His nose brushed her ear, as he softly growled, "God, how I want you!"

She pushed back into him, tipped her head back, and whispered, "I'm all yours."

He hungrily kissed her wanting lips.

She had been incorrigible, and he wasn't about to disappoint.

Aggressively they went at each other, pealing clothes off, kissing, nibbling, grabbing, touching; Cal swept her up into his arms and carried her back upstairs, to bed.

Katie released his anticipation from the restraints of his jeans. Taking a firm hold of his ridged erection, she teased him with her lips and tongue.

Cal's gray eyes flared intensely with need, and want. He couldn't take much more of Katie's teasing. Lifting her off her knees and lying her down on the bed, he ached to have her; gliding a hand up the inside of her warm silky thigh to find her ready.

Wrapping her legs around Cal, Katie playfully grabbed his face and nipped his bottom lip.

Giving in to the moment, Cal slowly entered his wanting Love, seating himself fully inside her.

A release of pleasure escaped her lips in a soft moan as he filled her.

With all the stress and pressures Cal had been dealing with, lying here with Katie gave him a chance to reflect and escape, at least for a little while. "Now that's a great way to start the day!" He kissed Katie's forehead and held her tighter.

*

This morning Katie and Billie met for breakfast at the Sci-Fi Café. The café's owner, Mary, was an author and had been researching the strange and unusual happenings in and around the Burlington area for over

15-years. She was aware of the tunnels, but had never been able to find an entrance to get in and explore them for herself.

Katie McGuire hired by her college mentor, Architect Paul Richter, to research the chipped white-brick building at 480 Milwaukee Avenue, had only begun to discover the history of this building. With the help of her good friend, Billie Jo, the two photographed and diagramed each floor of the abandoned 3-story building.

On the top floor, they uncovered a hidden space in the floor they suspected at one time held a safe; except for an old poker chip, it had been empty. In a beautifully carved wooden column by the bar they discovered a pneumatic capsule transport, from the Victorian era. Also, the measurements for the top two floors did not match the bottom floor. There was something off about these spaces. Katie suspected there was more to this building.

Kate had remained quite curious about all the boarded up rooms on the second floor; rooms that had been sealed up for decades. After Billie found an old red-leather diary under the floorboards in one of these rooms, they had another mystery to solve. When they realized the diary had belonged to a woman of ill repute; they were determined to find out what happened to its author.

On the first floor the girls had inadvertently found a concealed door to the building's basement. Behind the racks holding dusty bottles of wine, they discovered an entrance to a tunnel system under Burlington. No one seemed to know anything about these tunnels, including the Historical Society.

The girls took it upon themselves to explore the tunnels. Although some of these tunnels had collapsed or had been blocked, in others they found an underground bowling alley, and hidden rooms, which led them to expose the location of a Meth lab belonging to the biker gang, 7 Sons of Sin. The gang had also used a space under the floor in one of the tunnel's rooms to hide a cache of stolen military weapons. There was so much more to these tunnels that had not yet been discovered.

Only Kelly "Midas" Green, the homeless man who lived in the tunnels, knew another terrible secret these tunnels held. Midas had come home from Afghanistan, but not to the realities he knew prior to the war.

The explosion that imploded City Hall threatened to reveal the treacherous secret Midas had tried to keep hidden away.

When Billie showed Mary the diary they found, Mary shared what she knew. Mary eagerly flipped through it, as the girls ate, occasionally making comments to some of the book's content. "This building was the Burlington Hotel, and later the Plush Horse! That means Sadie was living here, in one of the rooms upstairs when this was a speakeasy!" Mary's tone was one of excitement. "Hold on – I have a letter that was sent to me by someone who lived here as a little girl, and she recalled playing in the tunnels. She also mentions a hidden room down there!" Mary got up to fetch the letter.

Mary soon returned, handing Katie the letter.

Katie's skin tingled with goose bumps as she read it. "She's describing exactly what we saw down there!"

Billie took a look at the letter, too. "She describes the rooms down there, just as we saw them!"

"I'd love to get back down there to really check out the tunnels!" Katie gave Billie a sideways glance; her tone was somewhat forlorn, "If they haven't collapsed already!"

Billie understood Katie's curiosity, but respected Jack's warning about going back down alone. Billie wouldn't let her friend go by herself; however, that didn't stop her from worrying about what else they might find.

*

Washington, D.C.

Lying as if asleep in the cool dewy grass, the perfectly groomed and manicured, well-toned body of a young woman was found by a jogger. Even with the early morning light Agent Mason Stone could see how beautiful she had been. Her lovely face was eerily peaceful.

Agent Stone crouched next to the woman's lifeless body. There was something hauntingly familiar in the way she had been boldly displayed and posed.

Twenty-four hours later, his suspicion of her being a high-end escort would be correct. Her body was flawless. No scars, or tattoos; rare for the younger generation today. Apart from the ligature marks behind her left ear, there was no indication she had been murdered. The only thing different from the last one is what the M.E. found. He pointed out a microchip imbedded in the back of her neck at the hairline.

"Huh - that's new?" Mason pondered his next move.

*

With the lights turned low, and snuggled up on the leather sofa with a glass of wine, Katie worried about Cal. Being in his arms felt so right, but there was something missing, he was distracted.

Everyone's mood seemed to be somber at best. It had only been a couple of weeks; however, Burlington was still recovering from the wake of destruction and loss left behind by Mayor Dunn. The shock of it all kept the rumor mill in motion.

The Village took their sweet time removing Police Chief Perry, keeping the investigation of his involvement close to the vest. Inquires were being made and everything the Chief had done over the past 3-years was being scrutinized. With the Mayor's absence and questions about their Chief, the police department was walking on eggshells.

The Village couldn't take the embarrassment, and Chief Perry wasn't about to go easily. He stubbornly refused to reinstate Detective Cal Chapman to duty after the shooting.

It was a sore subject right now for Cal, so Katie kept their conversation to the research she was doing on the 480 building. "I finished the floor plans for the building, and I discovered that the second and third floor measurements don't quite match the first floor. I believe there is a hidden passage from the third floor down."

"I *know* you want to go back down into those tunnels."

Katie coyly looked up into Cal's steely grey eyes.

"Don't give me that look!"

With a twinkle in her impish green eyes she flashed him a playful smile.

Before he could respond, the electronic leash he placed on the table loudly vibrated across the surface of its polished wood top. Taking a breath, he reached out for his phone. His brows furrowed when he saw the caller's number. "Chapman!" he answered as he stood.

Katie sat up now that her comfy position on the couch had been disrupted. She took a long sip of wine as she tried not to eavesdrop, but Cal was hesitant and short on the phone.

"That can't be right."

"Yes - of course."

"I can..."

"Let me make some arrangements and I'll get back to you."

Cal's tone was vague and short, and then he hung up. He stood holding his phone with a strange look on his face.

"Is everything alright?"

"Yeah - just a ghost from my past making a resurrection."

"What?"

"That was Mason Stone, my partner from the FBI. He's asked for my help on a case that's almost identical to *my* last one. He thinks it's the same guy. Mason wants me to come to D.C."

"Well, you're going to go, right?"

Cal cocked his head to Kate's words.

"Cal, if he thinks you can help him, maybe you should."

Thinking, he absently nodded his head yes, and walked out of the room. She could hear him climb the stairs.

She left him alone for while, and soon wondered what he was doing. Katie poured another glass of wine before heading upstairs. Reaching the upstairs hallway, she saw the attic door was ajar.

Cal had been digging through old case file boxes, and found for what he was searching for. If he was distracted before, Mason's call knocked him back into the past.

Taking a sip of wine, Katie watched Cal for a few moments. "Hey, are you okay?"

"Kate, I *need* to go to D.C."

Chapter 1

It had been three days since Cal left for D.C., and except for Hondo, Cal's German Sheppard, the Victorian was too quiet. She finally invited Billie over for some company. Settling in on the large leather sofa with a bottle of wine, Katie poured a glass for Billie as she started to read the diary aloud.

"The only thing I have left from my mother is her Bible. She used to read it to me. Now, when I read it, it has a different relevance than when I was a child. I am a sinner, but I can live with that. I am also a survivor.

My mother died when I was 13. My father wasn't much of a father after that. He'd drown his sorrow with corn whiskey most every night. At first, I'd worry about him making it home from wherever he'd be; but when he was home, he was a nasty drunk. The man I once knew and loved as my father, was now a stranger to me. That first year he was just angry and yelled a lot but was relatively harmless.

On the second anniversary of my mother's death, he came home drunk out of his mind. My pen shakes as I write this. That was the first night he came into my bed. That man I used to know as my father forced me to have relations with him. I hurt so badly. I remember how hard I cried. I could never look at him the same again.

After the first time, he didn't touch me again for a month. But something would set him off at work and he'd get drunk, and take his anger out on me. It discussed me. I hated him. Sometimes while I lay there just staring at a blank spot on the ceiling or wall, he'd stop and start to cry. He'd get off of me and leave, closing my door behind him. I got so I was numb to what was happening. No, this man wasn't my father. I believe my father died with my mother.

For two years he took me. The day I turned 16, I waited for him to leave the house. I packed a small suitcase, stole all the money he had stashed away in a sock drawer, took my mother's Bible and left.

I never looked back. I have to admit, it was bold and daring for anyone, especially for a 16-year-old girl who now had no one; until I met Viola."

Billie finished reading the passage from the diary and found Katie with tears in her eyes. "I'm sorry, Katie...I didn't mean to bring up any bad memories."

"I know that. These are Sadie's words, but we were both betrayed by men we loved. I'm okay, keep reading."

Billie reached out for Katie's hand and smiled.

Switching positions and settling in, Billie continued with Sadie's story.

"My best friend is Viola Cummings, but I call her Vi. We met at the train station. I had been staring at the departure board for a long time, trying to figure out where to go. I must have looked lost or maybe, just desperate.

She caught me looking at her. I recall her warm smile. She wasn't much older than I, but sure seemed much more confident and worldly.

'Hello, I'm Viola. What's your name Sugar?'

'Sadie.'

'Where ya headed, Sadie?

Looking to the Bible in my hands I said, 'To Hell for sure.'

I was quite serious, but she just laughed. Looking me over, 'Come with me.'

I was very skeptical and asked where.

'Well, as long as you know where you're headed, let's see if you can't have some fun along the way! But first, it looks like you could use a good meal and perhaps freshen up a bit? Yes?'

I don't know why I went with this stranger, but I did. I picked up my small case and followed Vi to Wisconsin.

For all the progression of the 1920's, there was still some very stupid social etiquette norms. Like coloreds and whites don't mix and don't even get me started on the Catholics.

I found it all to be just silly. I'm not much for rules, spoken or otherwise. Not then and not now.

Vi was a mulatto. She told me her momma was black and her daddy was white. People don't like races mixing, and some men killed her daddy because of it.

She and I made fast friends. She is as close to me as a sister could be. I don't worry what others think. Viola could be purple for all I care. She is my one true friend.

Vi introduced me to Hazel. A very large woman, who ran a cat-house called the Plush Horse in this town of Burlington, Wisconsin.

Viola worked and lived here at the Plush Horse and helped me to get a job working as a waitress. The pay wasn't much, but I was running out of coin from my sock. Vi let me bunk with her, but things got difficult when she'd have clients. I would have to sit outside the door or down in the lobby and wait for her to be finished.

Although Vi was a mulatto, she passed for an exotic woman from someplace far away. This alone made it okay for a white man to bed her and not have the stigma of bedding a colored.

I really can't say exactly how I got started whoring. But the first time, I remember I cried. I couldn't help it. The man got angry, slapped me around and demanded his money back, or a different whore. 'One that could at least pretend to like it', were his words.

Hazel was hopping mad.

Vi came to speak to me afterwards. She educated me as to the ways of the world and men. 'No matter what, always be a lady!' she would say. 'How they treat you don't say anything about who you are, and everything about who they are.'

Billie paused. "Do you want me to stop reading?"

Katie was quiet, but shook her head, "No, keep reading."

Billie had read this diary before, but now reading it aloud with Katie, the story took on a different perspective.

"Katie, I can tell it's bothering you. We can read some more tomorrow."

Chapter 2

1920's

A subtle breeze kicked out a sail. The long curve of taught white canvas was a strong contrast to the brilliant blue of the sky with barely a wisp of a cloud. Dark navy rolled out as far as the eye could see. The lull of the sea's slow rhythmic waves slapped against *West Wind Reverence's* hull was tranquil, until the cry of an occasional gull pierced the serenity. The salty sea air filled Cliff's lungs; crisp and refreshing.

The incredibly sharp, handsome and debonair, Clifford Westbrook was a quiet man who enjoyed listening to the Victrola, or reading classic novels. He tried to keep to himself, away from all the pomp and pressures of being a Westbrook. Being an avid sailor, he took out his Knockabout Sloop every chance he got. It was the only way he could find some solitude.

Sailing gave Cliff the freedom to ponder the things most important to him, letting his thoughts of greater things to come drift out on calm waves.

The Westbrooks had settled in New York from England in the 1800's, established themselves as shipping tycoons, and even owned a paper mill. They had two homes, a modest mansion on the Gold Coast, off Long Island's north shore, and one in Poughkeepsie.

Socializing with the upper echelon of high society, including Marshall Field and the Vanderbilts; the Westbrooks had money, *old money,* and lots of it. However, Cliff always wanted to make his own way in life.

Although born into the upper crust, Clifford Westbrook was never truly impressed with uninhibited wealth and opulence. He believed, flamboyantly showing it off was distasteful and was more interested in what one could accomplish with that kind of wealth. There were too many unwritten rules, social and otherwise. It was exhausting trying to live-up to being a Westbrook. Growing up, Cliff's family dragged him to all the élite social gatherings, which he detested. It was Cliff's obligation to entertain the hosts' daughter or niece. There *were* a couple he actually liked, they were smart, and had something to say; but, for the most part the girls were attractive, spoiled, and self-absorbed empty shells. Cliff wasn't interested in these superficial young ladies who flaunted over him, certainly not enough to formally court any of them.

Standing up to his father, departing on his own terms, Clifford Westbrook studied medical sciences at Oxford. Upon his return home to the States, there were standing offers at some of the top research facilities in the nation. To get as far away from his family as he could, he took a job on the west coast, working on elements and their effects on plants, animals and humans. He followed the findings of John Yiamouyiannis, whose research overlapped his own. Shortly after earning his PhD, Cliff received a job offer in Chicago he couldn't refuse.

These were exciting times. Not only did prosperity grow across the country, but there was a shared feeling with the booming modern technologies that anything could be possible.

Cliff was ready to strive for more. Once in Chicago, Cliff met Jonathan Blake. Blake, like Westbrook was at the top of his field. Although Jonathan was a good 20-years Cliff's senior, the pair hit it off famously.

Cliff was enthusiastic with the prospect of working alongside Dr. Blake. Blake was already established and well respected as a scientist. There was much Cliff could learn from him.

Cliff also learned very quickly that Blake had two sides. At work, he was the hardworking straightforward and daring scientist. While work was thrilling for him in its own right, outside of work, he was a big kid who enjoyed life to its fullest. Jonathan wasn't quite the ladies-man, although athletically built, he was more awkward than suave. He had a dry sense of humor, and at times could have a quick temper.

Blake worked hard and played even harder. He made it his mission, to introduce his new partner to all the hot spots in the City of Chicago. There was no better way to cut loose.

After all - this was the era of breaking with traditions. Women were wearing make-up, cut their hair short, and wore dresses that showed off their knees as they danced. Even more daring, women now smoked and drank in public.

This was an era where Jazz meant freedom, and life moved fast. In Chicago, life was one big party. At night, the city came alive with parties, drink and music. Musicians flocked to Chi-town, with the likes of Earl Hines, Al Jolson, Louis Armstrong and Paul Whiteman. They had a sound all their own. While the Jazz music from New Orleans was wild, almost primitive sounding; Chicago jazz was more uniformed, almost polite. Cliff appreciated this new sound very much.

Prohibition wasn't slowing anyone down, either. The Chicago outfit, run by Al Capone kept the hooch flowing in every speakeasy and gambling house. Usually, the higher the cover charge, the better quality of booze.

They had three favorite joints where they liked to go. One was the Drake Hotel, it was pretentious and reminded Cliff too much of what he left at home. The second was the Green Mill, owned by Al Capone's man, "Machine Gun" Jack McGurn. A couple of times they even saw Capone there. The Dreamland Cafe, a black and tan jazz club, was Cliff's all time favorite.

Though racial tensions ran high after The Great War, the middle and upper class whites still didn't want their kids listening to colored music, *Jazz.* Frankly, neither Jonathan nor the aristocratic Clifford gave a damn what society dictated. They didn't carry the same prejudices.

Tonight, they ventured out to the Dreamland Cafe.

A hard knock on the back door signaled the doorman to open the little hatch in the door.

Peeking through a small window, Jon gave a password, and then slipped a Jackson to the large gorilla wearing a fedora and a gun strapped under his suit coat, allowing them access.

The smoky cafe was filled with a lively buzz, and lots of chatter. Cliff followed Jon up to the bar. Even though it was tightly packed, they managed to squeeze in to order a couple of drinks. Never truly sure if they were pouring good Canadian whiskey or rot-gut, it was always a safer bet to order mixed drinks, "Two, whiskey Old Fashions!"

A hush fell upon the bar as soon as the intoxicating woman on stage began to sing. Her powerful yet sexy bluesy voice radiated throughout the room. Cliff's attentions quickly turned to the talented young woman on stage. She was a petite thing, with flawless skin the color of creamed coffee, and the most exquisite dark amber eyes. Her lips and nails painted the same color of vermilion. Her Champaign beaded sheath dress hung softly against her curves, glistening and reflecting facets of light.

"That canary has a set of pipes on her!" Jon smiled, as he elbowed Cliff. "She's a real looker, too!"

A roar of applause and whistles erupted when she finished. Her heavily beaded dress made little clacking sounds as she made her way down front to a small booth where another young woman sat. Men seemed to gravitate to them.

After her second performance, Cliff decided he was going to make her acquaintance. He was used to women coming to him, but here in Chicago, he was in unfamiliar territory. Now, standing in front of their table, he realized the two prettiest dames in the club, were seated before him; one white and one of color. They were an odd pair for the time.

The dolls graciously smiled back at the handsome man.

"Good evening, ladies! Do you mind if my friend and I join you?"

The pair giggled.

"And which friend would that be?" Asked the strawberry-haired beauty as her flirtatious blue eyes twinkled.

Sensing that he was standing alone, he looked back to the bar, and waved Jonathan over.

The sharp-dressed man ambled over and stood next to him, "Ladies, this is my good friend Jon, and I am Cliff." He said, smiling warmly.

The exotic beauty smiled back, "Hello, this is Sadie, and I'm Viola, but you can call me Vi!" Her sultry undertones were anything but subtle.

The girls moved in, so the men could join them. Ordering a round of drinks from their cocktail waitress, 2-more whiskey Old Fashions, a Manhattan, and Viola ordered a Martini; *"dirty - very dirty with extra olives".*

The talented Viola may have interested Cliff at first; however, as the night progressed, the more he took notice of Sadie.

Sadie had a very genuine quality, one of those gals who was as beautiful on the inside as she was on the outside. Her incredible light-blue eyes were a striking contrast to her soft strawberry-colored hair. She had an infectious smile, and Cliff loved to hear her laugh. He could tell Sadie was well read, and soon found himself intensely engaged in lively conversation with her, almost forgetting where he was or who was with them. A charming lady with a tender heart, but there was more to Sadie; something she kept guarded. A quiet strength that even she didn't know she had, but he saw it. Cliff was surely love-struck.

Couples danced the Lindy, the Charleston and the Fox Trot just letting themselves go in the moment. Sadie and Cliff had a grand time dancing. Cliff, who was used to more formal dances, was smooth and light on his feet. While Jon was not so limber, Vi was highly amused teaching him a dance or two.

Cliff perceived Viola to be a bit more street-wise, and quite protective of Sadie.

Although both Jon and Cliff continued to be complete gentlemen, and thoroughly enjoyed the company of these ladies; the sultry Viola cautiously directed the evening. When the evening came to an end, Vi remained charming, yet politely refused a ride to the train station.

Cliff was not accustomed to allowing women to go unescorted. He insisted on dropping them off.

"That would be keen!" smiled Sadie as she grabbed hold of Cliff's arm.

Sadie's smitten expression caved Vi's resolution. She had never seen Sadie so joyful.

Cliff brought his car around. The cream and black 2-tone 1926 Rickenbocker Super Sport Coupe was a real head-turner. Long and sleek, it could easily do 100 mph.

Opening the suicide door, Jon climbed in the back seat with Vi, while Cliff came around and held the door open for Sadie. She happily slid into the front seat. As Sadie settled in to the rich leather seat, she ran an admiring hand over the beautiful smooth Teak-wood dash, resembling that of an airplane's cockpit. Cliff climbed in behind the wheel. He gave Sadie a side-ways glance to see she had already been eyeing him. He smiled and gave her a little wink.

The past few hours had been incredible, but now the reality that he might never see Sadie again, left Cliff feeling empty.

Pulling up to Union Station, the men got out first to hold the car doors open for the ladies.

Cliff offered Sadie his hand to help her out of the car. Her bright eyes locked onto his. He pulled her in close and kissed her full on the mouth. Impulsive for Cliff, yet he didn't want her to just fade away into the early morning light.

"I'd like to see you again, Miss Sadie."

She smiled wide, "You just might!" she said as she turned to walk away.

Just like that, the two women skipped down the stairs into the belly of Union Station and were gone.

All that remained was the flavor of Sadie's cherry lip stain on Cliff's lips, and he joyfully smiled.

Chapter 3

Burlington, Wisconsin, January 1928.

The air was bitter cold, and the skies were gray. The frozen streets were lined with roadsters, coupes and Model-A Fords with their wide running boards, spoke wheels, and white-walls. Most of the cars were Phoenix brown, deep maroon or gun-metal blue, and some even had two-tone harmonies.

Ahooga!

Their funny little horns sounded at each other or passersby.

Wide dark green and white striped awnings covered entrances. Three-piece suits in brown, navy or gray topped with felt Fedoras beckoned in a haberdashery window front. In the window next door, the latest in women's fashion was displayed. A couple women with pin curls exited the dress shop carrying dress boxes.

As the black sedan drove Dr. Westbrook through town, everyone on the street cautiously watched them as they passed. It's not every day a dark sedan comes to town; and when it does, there is usually trouble.

The big sedan turned onto Jefferson Street and made its way to the back of a 3-story white-brick building. The driver got out and opened the door for Dr. Clifford Westbrook. Dr. Blake was already there waiting with another gentleman. His uptight, rigid appearance told Cliff, *this* was their new boss.

Dr. Blake introduced Dr. Clifford Westbrook to Mr. Jeremy Nickels. The men shook hands in greeting.

Mr. Nickels made an open handed gesture, "Please, Dr. Blake, shall we?"

The men entered through a door leading into the Western Union. Passing through a small lobby there was a colored man shining shoes. His smile was friendly as he nodded to them in passing. They took a side door that opened to a narrow staircase, which led them down below the 480 building.

A dark, non-descript looking office was set up to receive only *special* visitors, and an armed guard stood vigilant at the door behind the receptionist. None of this felt right to Cliff. He was expecting a more modern facility; one without the cloak and dagger presence.

Jonathan exchanged a weary glance with Cliff. At that moment he was waiting for Cliff to express his '*I told you so!*'

Through the door, Cliff and Jonathan followed Mr. Nickels to the left, into a dimly lit hallway made of brick and mortar.

The clinic's office was already established, and staffed. The few that were there, although none of them were in uniform, Cliff could tell by their mannerisms and statures they were military personnel.

The group passed another secured vault-like door.

Cliff spoke up, "What's through there?"

"Not of your concern - but in due time, Dr. Westbrook." Niceties aside, Mr. Nickels was cold, abrupt, and to the point. Definitely a government man.

Cliff gave Jon a sideways glance.

In their office, the filing cabinets were already filled with case studies and documented research from others who had been here before them. There was much to do before they could even pick up where the others had left off.

Mr. Nickels escorted them back to reception.

On queue the receptionist handed over a brown interpersonal envelope with a big red stamp across the front of it. "That concludes our tour." He unwound its string, retrieving credentials for both doctors. "You will need these to gain access to restricted areas. Keep these with you at all times. Dr. Blake will show you where you'll be staying while working on Project Zephyr. Let me remind you, this is classified. You are not to share what you see, hear or do. I will keep in touch so you can keep me apprised of your progress."

Mr. Nickel's turned on his heels to leave, but stopped short. He turned back with another direct order. "And gentlemen, nothing is to leave this facility. Any of your findings will remain with us. Do I make myself clear?"

Jonathan glared in Mr. Nickel's direction, while Clifford answered. "Understood."

They watched their new boss climb the steps and exit right.

Jon exhaled, "Let's get you settled, shall we?"

"Lead the way." Cliff wanted to say more. Much more; however, this was neither the time nor place. They knew from now on everything they said or did would be scrutinized.

Once again passing through the lobby Cliff noticed the kindly shoeshine man. Making eye contact he tipped his hat to the man.

The man smiled and nodded in turn, as Cliff followed Jon out.

The brisk winter air hit Cliff in the face, making his eyes suddenly water. The wind whipped around the corner and dove straight down his collar. He hitched up his shoulders to his ears and folded over the deep lapels of his woolen over coat. "So where are we going?"

"You're actually right here." Jon said as he looked up to the windows above them. "They have you staying at the Badger Hotel, its right next door. The 480 building we just left had some major renovations done in '23. It used to only be a 2-story, but they raised it to add more rooms to this hotel. Except you and I both know what they were really doing."

"If I'm staying here, where are you staying?"

"My son and his family live in town, so I'm staying with them."

"You have family here?"

"I sure do! I've been so entrenched with my research, I've lost touch." Jon's voice trailed off, as he looked down the street.

Cliff sensed there was something there he didn't want to discuss and allowed him to drop it.

Jon escorted Cliff up to his room. His suitcase was already waiting for him. Cliff strode to the window and peered out. "What did we agree to, Jon?"

Jon stood hat in hand not sure how to answer.

Looking back over his shoulder, Cliff said, "I don't trust this Nickels fella."

"Well, tomorrow we will be able to start looking through all those files.   Why don't you relax?   Get yourself settled in."

The door closed behind Jon.

Cliff turned back to gaze out the window to the cold dampened streets below. Jonathan appeared as he exited the hotel, and Cliff watched him stroll down the sidewalk until he was out of sight.

Burlington was a quaint little town, with its delightful brick buildings and Midwest charm. But there was something else going on here. Something dark and secretive. Cliff didn't like going into things blindly, and this would be no exception. Starting tomorrow, he was going to learn everything he could about Project Zephyr, and what it was they were actually doing for the War Department.

Chapter 4

The next morning, eager to start, Jon rapped on Cliff's door, and was surprised when the door opened instantly.

Cliff, too, was anxious to start digging through files.

Entering the lobby of the 480 building, they were greeted with a friendly smile from the shoeshine man. He nodded in Cliff's and Jon's direction.

Before ducking down the stairs to their new place of business, Cliff returned the pleasant smile and nodded in turn.

A pretty brunette sat behind the desk wearing a serious uptight look upon her face. She glanced up in acknowledgement as the two scientists walked past.

Jon could never just pass by a pretty face. He smiled in her direction and gave her a wink; holding the brunette's gaze a little longer than she liked.

The stern hulk of a man guarding the egress into the tunnels kept stoic as he glanced at their IDs, eyed them both, and then stepped aside.

The second time Cliff entered these tunnels leading to his office wasn't any more settling than the first. Dimly lit bulbs in tin housing hummed and illuminated their way.

Their office was sparsely furnished, but all they really needed were two desks and the files. Someone had made coffee already filling the room with a rich warm aroma.

Jon poured two cups and handed one to Cliff.

"Shall we get started? You take one drawer I'll take the next."

Jon agreed, pulling out a handful of folders; making a grunting sound as he sat down in the wooden desk chair. Jon pulled out his wire-rimmed specks, resting them on the end of his nose, took a swig of coffee and opened the first folder.

Cliff's first case file quickly caught his attention. They had been researching the 9th element on the periodic table, Fluorine. He was perplexed, "What were these scientists doing with Fluorine?"

"Well, that's what we're supposed to figure out."

"He said *classified*, Jon. How do they deem any of this classified?"

What wasn't blacked out line by line in the notes was barely legible, and difficult to decipher. Making his own notations from what he read, Cliff didn't know what to make of these research files. From the content of Dr. Rourk's findings to those of Dr. Meils', one could determine the positive results were much weaker than the negative ones.

By the time Cliff had finished reading through most of the first drawer, he was exhausted. His eyes burned and his mind was spinning. He pinched the bridge of his nose as he hung his head.

It was going painstakingly slow, and took them all day to get through one drawer.

Jon looked up and found Cliff in need of a break. "I say let's call it a day. Time for a stiff one, my friend!"

"I don't know, Jon."

"Trust me; the booze will relax that big brain of yours!"

Cliff considered the tone behind Jon's boyish grin, "I should have known you've already found every gin joint in town."

Jon's grin only grew.

*

Tonight wasn't any different than any other night. The Plush Horse was a favorite gin joint in town, with the added benefit of having the girls for entertainment upstairs. It wasn't like the eloquent speakeasies 80-miles south in Chicago, but it wasn't a Blind Pig either.

The dance music played, while the bathtub gin and Canadian whiskey flowed. The bar was filled with high-spirited, happy people mingling, partying and dancing the night away. Some of the painted gals started a petting party right in the lobby.

Though the night's mirth was in full swing, it was time for the girls to retire up to their rooms. The lottery had been drawn, and they needed to service the lucky men who drew their keys.

Sitting at the bar with Jon, Cliff caught a whiff of a familiar fragrance. Looking up into the bar's mirror he looked for the woman to whom it belonged. From across the room, Cliff got a glimpse of strawberry-hair. Quickly turning around to take a better look at the woman, but in that instant she was gone. He closed his eyes and shook the faint memory from his mind. After all, that was back in Chicago, months ago. She couldn't possibly be here, in Burlington, Wisconsin of all places.

A hotsy-totsy cocktail waitress pedaling delectable concoctions wove through the guests. Jon snatched a drink off the gal's tray. Scoping out the joint he took a large drink, "No, it's not Chicago, but it'll do!"

"I suppose Burlington has its own charm." Cliff took a sip from his drink.

Jon laughed, "I sure do miss Chicago!"

Upstairs in room-5, Viola, one of the Plush Horse's favorites, had fluffed and prepped for her next rube; the men never left her parlor disappointed. Lounging on the turned down bed, her ample charms waited for the next one.

Across the hall in room-4, sweet Sadie striped down to her fancy undergarments. She may have been a whore, but she still had some modesty. She had a process; numbing herself, both mentally and physically, to the task at hand. Sex was sex. That was all. She detached herself from the reality of her job. It wasn't something she was proud of, but at least it was honest work.

A key inserted into a door's lock and turned, opening to a night of pleasure bought and paid for. The sound always brought a cold sharp pain to her chest; still she learned to put fears aside to work.

Back at the Badger Hotel, Cliff was distracted. It had been a mentally draining day, going over so much information in those files. Cliff now laid awake thinking of strawberry-hair, blue eyes, a beautiful smile, and an infectious laugh.

Chapter 5

Breakfast at the cafe was welcomed, realizing they had missed lunch yesterday and drank their dinner.

Cliff was quiet; pondering the sporadic information they were being fed.

This morning as they passed through the lobby of the 480 building, Cliff stopped to get his shoes shined.

"I'll be down shortly."

Jonathan simply furrowed his eyebrows and quietly continued on down through the non-descript wooden door.

Cliff took a seat in the empty shoeshine chair.

"G'd mornin'!" The shoeshine man said with a gregarious smile.

"Good morning!" Cliff returned the smile.

The man got busy cleaning and polishing Cliff's Hanan and Son brown leather cap toe shoes. The man worked in silence. There was no need to waste words.

Cliff was quite pleased with his work and would tip him well. "What's your name?"

"Nebraska, Sir!"

"Well, Nebraska, I'm Dr. Westbrook, but I want you to call me Cliff." He said with a friendly smile, as he handed Nebraska his coin and a little extra.

Wide-eyed, "Yes - Sir - Mr. Cliff! Thank you!"

Cliff smiled, picked up his fedora, draped his coat over one arm, giving Nebraska a nod before heading down to join his partner.

*

They eagerly devoured the information in the files; however, the deeper into them they searched, the nagging feeling of unrest took root.

They knew as early as the 1850's, the iron and copper industries were taking ore from the earth and removing the metal - which created airborne and waterborne fluorides that were poisoning people and livestock.

They found Fluorine to be the most reactive element known to science. In nature, it is found bonded to metallic ore and is safe. In its ionic state, Fluorine is highly toxic, and is difficult if not impossible to dispose of safely.

Most of the files had been blacked out, but the collective study showed that through the years, places where well-water had naturally high fluoride content, the people died at an early age from fluoride poisoning and other fluoride-related ailments. Among these hazards of fluoride were dental fluorosis (disintegrating), skeletal fluorosis, sterility, birth defects, cancer and brain damage.

As Cliff read these findings out loud, he was disgusted. "Tell me again, what we are to do with this information? What good can any of this do for the War Department?"

Jonathan shared a grave look with his partner. "We still have a few days worth of files to go through."

Piecing together the shreds of information gathered was of utmost importance. Cliff wasn't going to trust anything Mr. Nickels said, until he had a clearer picture of what had been previously done here. "I'm afraid we agreed to something we will regret."

*

Jon pushed himself away from his desk. "I need a break from all this. Let's get some fresh air...to clear our heads."

Cliff's observations made him suspicious about how the War Department could possibly use this information. He agreed, "Some fresh air sounds good."

They bundled up for the wintery weather, and trekked outside.

Jonathan's son's home was just a few blocks away. His daughter-in-law happily greeted them at the door. "Come in, I was just preparing lunch. Care to join us?"

"That would be great, Molly, thank you!" Jon answered for them both.

From the doorway of the dining room Jon's son, Charles cautiously watched the pair hang up their coats.

Cliff didn't feel Jon's son was as welcoming as his daughter-in-law.

They took seats around the kitchen table, as Molly served them chicken and rice soup with toasted cheese sandwiches.

Cliff enjoyed lunch very much; it reminded him of his youth and the lunches his nanny would prepare.

The coolness between Jon and his son was evident, but Cliff didn't want to pry.

Fed and content to get a fresh start, they walked back to the 480 building against the brisk winter wind. Cliff smiled and nodded to Nebraska, as he passed through the lobby.

Every day for weeks the same routine, check in, show IDs, and enter restricted tunnels. It was becoming redundant.

Dr. Blake, being Dr. Blake, liked to test the waters. Today was no different.

The receptionist, wearing her usual tight bun and a stern look watched Jon and Cliff closely.

The gate-keeper held steady, eyeing their IDs, before allowing them to pass.

"Do you gamble, Cliff?"

"I've played a fair hand of poker."

"Good - tonight, I think you and I shall check out Deuces!"

"Deuces?"

Jon pointed up, "The gambling house on the 3rd floor. Should be fun!"

Although the brunette wasn't in uniform, Jon gave her an impish grin and a wink, "Care to join us, Major? You can be my Lady Luck!"

To Cliff's surprise, he saw she fought the grin tugging at the corners of her mouth.

"Do you think flirting with her is wise?"

Slapping Cliff on the back, "Probably not, but she's got one hell of a chassis!" Jon jested. "Besides, that cool 'I'm ignoring you' stance she has is bullshit. She likes me...she just doesn't know it, yet."

"Must you be such a cad?"

Jon hiked-up his shoulders as he let Cliff's words roll off his back. "It's all part of my charm, son!" He chuckled.

"I think our definitions of 'charm', come from two entirely different books!"

*

After a month in Burlington, he decided this Saturday afternoon was a splendid time for Cliff to check out the town. Leaving the Badger Hotel heading south, he took in all the little shops, cafes and other businesses along Pine Street. He then cut over to head back north.

Passing through a crowd, a hint of perfume distracted Cliff. *Where do I know that scent?*

A distant memory of a woman kept his mind working until all hours of the night. *What was it about this mysterious woman?*

Chapter 6

Blacked out documents marked with random coffee stains littered the desk.

After weeks of grueling research, the frustrated Blake growled, "These don't tell us a damn thing!"

They had been at it for hours. Cliff checked his Patek Philippe; its time read 8:15. "Looks like we've worked through supper again."

Jon's face lit up, "Ready for a little fun?"

"I don't think so, not tonight."

"Aw don't be such a downer! There'll be chippies too; maybe one will help you take the edge off."

Cliff knew Jon needed to blow off some steam. Maybe he should go just to keep Jon from getting into too much trouble.

Cliff noticed Nebraska had already gone. The lobby was void from all activity. An eerie quietness followed them until they passed a few painted ladies, a few flirtatious winks, and smiles as they playfully rubbed passed the two men climbing the stairs up to the 3rd floor.

Jon led the way, knocking on the door at the top of the stairs. A short square-bodied Dago with dark slicked-back hair and shifty eyes greeted them. He looked them over before allowing them entrance.

A large wooden bar with ornate carved pillars on either side of the large bar mirrors was centered in the smoky room. Gaming tables filled the space with lots of activity. In the middle of it all, sat a distinguished looking man with dark eyes that quietly monitored the room.

A pretty blonde with long gams sheathed in dark patterned hosiery, directed Jon and Cliff to the game of their choice. Jon, of course, was eager to jump right in.

Cliff may have been raised in the upper crust of society; however, he understood gangsters and how they operated. Even in this small Midwestern town of Burlington, they were present. There was no doubt, Deuces was connected.

Seated at a poker table, Jon and Cliff played a few hands. Jon downed his drinks quickly. The more he drank the better he played. Cliff backed away from the drink and the table to keep a better eye on Jon.

Another round of drinks delivered by a sexy dame pushing-up more than adequate cleavage, only momentarily distracted Jon.

Jon reached out for the woman's arm before she could leave. With a scoundrel's grin he encouraged her to give him a good luck kiss. "Come on, Baby."

"Sorry Mac, the banks closed!" She snapped.

Blake laughed and tipped her with a chip.

"What a bearcat - I think I'm in love boys!"

Only a few chuckled at Jon's unruliness. The others didn't find him so funny. Blake was up quite a bit. The tensions around the table made Cliff uneasy. A new face, an intoxicated new face taking their money was stirring some dissention.

Cliff thought it was best they excused themselves from the table before they got the bums rush.

Feeling all eyes on them, Cliff got Jon motivated to call it a night and return another day.

Reluctantly, the block of a man at the door let them go; however, a subtle nod from the sinister looking man at the back of the room made it so.

*

Having slept off the night's folly in a chair, Dr. Blake was more owly than usual. Cliff insisted Jon drink some black coffee before going to work. An ornery Dr. Blake was better than not having him there at all.

Nebraska was at his usual spot in the lobby when they entered.

Cliff tipped his hat to Nebraska, "Good morning!"

"Morning, Mr. Cliff! Thought you's might want to know, you's got a visitor this morning."

"Thanks, Nebraska, I appreciate the heads up." Cliff passed the man a sawbuck, and smiled.

They found Mr. Nickels waiting for them in their office.

Jonathan grumbled under his breath, "Well, this can't be good."

Cliff engaged the man in black, "To what, do we owe this pleasure?"

Mr. Nickels' usual controlling and superior attitude was amplified this morning. "You've had sufficient time to sort through the files. Now you need to see something."

"Show us what - Sir?" Cliff questioned.

With a raised brow, Jonathan straightened up, "Do tell."

Mr. Nickels didn't care for Dr. Blake's attitude, but knew he was the best mind for the job. "Follow me, please."

They were led through a narrow passageway and down a few concrete steps to a sublevel. It was cool and damp down there.

Behind them, Cliff felt the presence of an armed guard following.

Nickels stopped just outside a wooden door with heavy iron hardware. "After the Great War, with the loss of lives, and men who came home not quite whole, we were determined to be prepared for anything. Gentlemen, it's not a matter of *if* there will be another war, it's *when*!"

Cliff and Jon shared a look.

"Dr. Blake and Dr. Westbrook, in our search to create a serum to build strength, or maybe help our soldiers heal faster...what they found did the exact opposite. In fact, the element they were working with was debilitating and catastrophic in so many ways. Most disturbing were the test subjects already showing signs of sickness, and death quickly became the end result."

"Excuse me, Mr. Nickels, you said test subjects?" Cliff inquired.

Mr. Nickels gave Dr. Westbrook a condescending sneer. "Yes, it is a necessary evil." Then he unlocked the door to allow them access.

The armed guard stayed behind, keeping his post just outside the door.

The smell of death and despair hung heavily in the air of the eerily quiet tomb-like space, lined on both sides with small prison-like cells.

Dr. Blake remained reticently quiet, as they took in all of the horrors they witnessed in each cell. A frightening realization washed over the scientists.

Cliff couldn't believe what they just witnessed. "Who are they?"

Mr. Nickels coolly answered, "All you need to know is that no one will ever miss them."

Quietly they exited the same way they had come. Mr. Nickels locked the door behind him. He proceeded back down the hall to the large vault door Cliff questioned the first day.

They passed through two archways before arriving at their new research lab. Here there were no guards, just a large heavy metal vault-like door stood in their way.

As Mr. Nickels swung the door open Cliff took notice of its thickness. Wondering to himself, for what exactly *did* he sign up?

Entering their lab for the first time was like stepping into the future. It was top notch, a dream come true for any scientist.

They stepped out onto a steel grid platform, holding onto the metal railing as they gaped at the vast white sterile static room before them. They looked down two levels. The dozen or so men in lab coats working on various equipment didn't bother to acknowledge their intrusion.

Mr. Nickels spoke, breaking the quiet void between them. "Gentlemen, in a race between two nations, research on human vulnerability has taken a turn. The USSR is already deep in parapsychological research. Controlling human behavior could potentially have major military benefits. What you see before you, is our think tank, our special research lab. These men like you are all a part of something greater. You will have unlimited funding and access to any equipment you desire. If something needs to be built, let us know."

There was something hidden in Mr. Nickels' words that Cliff couldn't grasp. What he was seeing somehow warped his own reality, "What exactly do you want of Dr. Blake and me? What is Project Zephyr?"

Mr. Nickels smugly answered, "I want to win that race, gentlemen. There are skeptics who would disagree, but in the future, not all weapons will be guns or bombs. It will be simple yet devastating. Let's see what you can do."

Things were now moving fast for the scientists. After years of research, Dr. Blake should be excited with what the prospect of unlimited funding could mean. However, what was just revealed to him made him question his part in this work.

Cliff was also cynical to say the least. He never thought the government should have anything to do with science. To him, science was knowledge, building and organizing that knowledge through testable explanations to a desired obtainable result. He strongly felt that anytime special interest groups (i.e. the government) get involved, the science becomes corrupt. The propaganda machines spin their lies until the truth no longer matters, only what those with the best propaganda want us to believe.

Cliff believed himself to be a patriot. He wanted to do good for the men who fought to protect this country. What he just witnessed wasn't the way.

Mr. Nickels' words didn't set right with either scientist, and throwing an ungodly amount of money into their lab didn't make them feel any better about it.

After everything they saw today, they needed a distraction. The two found themselves upstairs in Deuces, again. Although Cliff didn't care much for gambling; he did find some humor in watching Jonathan play.

Jon was brilliant; research and clinical studies weren't the only things Dr. Jonathan Blake excelled in. He knew his way around a poker table, even Black Jack.

Cliff figured Jon won as much as he drank - most nights breaking even. He wasn't really in it to get rich...just to have a bit of fun, and maybe tick-off those he played against.

Noticing Cliff wasn't having nearly as much fun as he was, Jon excused himself from the table. Bellying up to the bar he ordered another drink, "And one for my friend here, too." Jon then turned to Cliff, "You want to tell me what's eating you?"

Cliff looked down through the golden liquid to the bottom of his glass before taking the last swallow. Quietly, and with anger in his voice, "What we saw today?"

Jon got in Cliff's ear and growled, "*This* isn't the place to discuss it."

The bartender placed two drinks on the bar in front of them.

Cliff preferred keeping a clear head, and didn't care about having another drink.

"Look...don't let this change our commitment. Personally, I like challenges and would like to see how far we can take this."

Taking his drink, Cliff rolled the rocks glass between his hands with heavy thoughts.

Chapter 7

It was now almost March. Cliff stood at his hotel room window peering out to the streets below. People dashed into shops here and there. The purr of a car rolled down the street. Cliff was getting used to the melancholy flow of Burlington.

The faint glimpse of strawberry-hair peaking underneath a black felt cloche hat caught his eye. His heart skipped a beat with the mere thought of the delightful Sadie in Chicago. Cliff barely knew Sadie, but here he was thinking about her, again. Many times he wondered what ever happened to her. He and Jon had returned to the Dreamland Café hoping to find her there, but never did. Thinking of her put a smile on his face. He decided, today was going to be a good day.

*

After dinner, Cliff took an evening stroll. The fresh air would do him a world of good after spending so much time underground. He wondered if anyone in town *really knew* what was right under their noses.

The happy sounds of women laughing and talking made their way up the alley way and onto the street. Cliff heard their laughing as he walked past the alley. There was a very distinctive laugh. He stopped and took a step back. That's when he caught another glimpse of strawberry-hair. It was but a brief moment before the woman stepped out of view.

Just the sight of a woman with strawberry-hair made his heart pulsate a little quicker. He didn't think it could be possible, but *that* laugh, was *her* laugh. He could never forget Sadie's laugh. With a little bit of wishful thinking and high hopes he ventured down the alley in search of a strawberry-haired beauty.

The voices had quieted as Cliff neared the back of the buildings. The sound of a door closed and then, silence. His hopes faded.

Cliff emerged from the alley behind the brick buildings. He looked around trying to figure out where she could have gone. The closest door was the back entrance of a speakeasy, the Plush Horse. *"Maybe?"* He thought.

Taking a chance he ducked inside. He found a couple of gal's sitting on gentlemen's laps. No dancing or gaiety, just some drinking and a little necking. The mood inside was relatively quiet. To his disappointment, no strawberry-haired beauty. After a somber walk-through Cliff headed back to his hotel.

He couldn't get Sadie off his mind. A restless night of dreaming about *her,* and it was back to the lab.

Distracted with visions of Sadie, Cliff entered the 480 building lost in thought.

Nebraska was polishing a man's shoes. He turned to smile and nod in Cliff's direction.

Cliff only gave a subtle nod in turn before heading down.

Nebraska took notice, but simply turned back to his customer.

The large guard allowed Cliff to pass.

Dr. Blake was already in the office with a cup of Java.   He noticed Cliff's mood and frowned at his demeanor. "Want to talk about it?"

Cliff absently poured himself a cup, "There's nothing to talk about." Steam danced from the dark hot brew as he lightly blew across the top before taking a sip.

Jon knew something was on Cliff's mind, but let it drop. "Good - I want to show you something."

With mild interest Cliff followed Jon. When they passed by the lab, he was a bit confused, "Where are we going?"

In a hushed voice Jon answered, "Just be quiet, follow me and proceed like you have the authority to go where we're going!"

They continued past where the vaulted ceilings intersected. The dimly lit tunnel was but an empty void. Only the sound of their feet shuffling along filled the space.

Jon slowed, and then paused in front of an iron gate.

Cliff looked on as Jon picked its lock.

A sharp click broke the silence.

"I see you have another skill."

Jon simply shrugged. "It's a gift."

Cliff slipped in, waiting for Jon to cautiously close the heavy iron gate behind them.

"This way." Jon motioned for Cliff to follow.

Cliff was in awe of the extent in which these tunnels stretched under the town of Burlington.

There were metal grates in the walls further down. Cliff took a peek through one that had a soft light beyond it. It was a room; a small quiet room with a safe that sat in the corner behind a wooden door, directly across from where he peered. In the center of the room stood a table with 3-chairs around it.

With a finger to his lips, Jon tugged on Cliff's sleeve to encourage him to move along.

First Jon led him north. This tunnel came up into a sub-basement of the grainery. There was a room separate from the main basement. Here there were many bottles of wine, and a large crude-looking vat. The fumes were heady, and Cliff could only imagine how the wine tasted. "What is this place?"

"Your colored friend has a hobby."

"Nebraska, makes wine?"

"I watched him bottle that batch over there last night. He didn't see me. I kept to the shadows."

"Why were you spying on Nebraska?"

"I wasn't. I've been staying late just so everyone would get tired of waiting around for me to leave. When they finally left...I take a look around down here. I've been down 3-tunnels so far. I just thought this might interest you."

"Where else do the tunnels go?"

"The one south of here goes east to the river and comes out right by the Theater."

"That room you peered into - I've seen that mean-looking fella from Deuces counting money. There's something else I want to show you, but it'll have to wait. We need to head back before they realize we're missing."

Cliff's eyes were quite open. This quaint little town hid many secrets. He thought about how the townsfolk were clueless to what was really happening right under their noses. Although most knew about the gambling, prostitution and of course the bootleg, they just didn't speak of it. But what would they say if they knew about the hidden government research facility conducting lethal experiments on people?

Cliff had real doubts about the project on which they were working, and it wore heavily on his conscience.

*

Once again they had worked through dinner. Cliff looked at his partner and could see the stress in his face. Looking to his wristwatch, "Jon, I think it's time we get out of here. You look like you could use a drink, and have a bit of fun."

"You don't have to twist my arm! The Plush Horse?"

Cliff smiled. It was as if Jon had read his mind. "Sounds good."

It didn't take long for some blonde kitten drinking "giggle water" to attach herself to Jon. With her on his lap, Cliff could see him quickly getting out of his funk.

Cliff found a table at the back of the room where he could survey the full scope of the joint. He couldn't get the thought of Sadie off his mind. He knew he heard her laugh. It was crazy to believe she here in Burlington of all places, but wishful thinking was all he had. Cliff found himself staring at the sexy exotic woman sitting at the bar. He couldn't believe his eyes. He recognized her. Surrounded by men, all pining to light her cigarette, was Vi.

Vi held out the long cigarette holder with a Lucky Strike fixed to it. Her high glossed vermilion lips left a smudge on the rim of her glass. Fishing out the speared olives from the empty drink, she glanced over in Cliff's direction. Her smoldering eyes gave him a wink with recognition.

Cliff's pulse quickened. A happy euphoria pulsed through his veins. If she was here, surly so was Sadie. He scanned the entire room for the lovely young Sadie. Remembering back to the night they met in Chicago, he could almost taste her cherry lipstick again.

Vi smiled in her charming way, "Pardon me fellas!" Slid down from her barstool and slinked through the small crowd to Cliff.

Always the proper gentleman, Cliff stood in the lady's presence.

"Well - well, what do we have here? Where's your friend, Jonny?" She asked as she craned her neck looking around for him.

Looking down at Vi, Cliff stood quite sober, though he felt like he was about to vibrate out of his skin.

"Aw shucks handsome - you looking for Sadie?"

"Is she here?" Trying not to sound, too anxious.

Vi cocked her head to one side and blew out a long drag from her Lucky Strike. "Sure, Honey, you'll just have to wait your turn! She'll be down soon enough." Cozying up to Cliff, Vi fingered his lapels, "In the meantime, how about you buy this gal a drink?"

The expression on his face told Vi he didn't know they were whores. "Aw shucks, Sugar - you didn't know - did ya?"

They shared an intense look. An erratic tidal wave of emotions cursed through him; soaring from an elated high then plummeting to a sudden low of shock, confusion, anger and disappointment. Cliff suddenly had many questions.

"Geez, I'm sorry toots! Come sit!" Vi looked back to the barkeep and signaled to bring two drinks over.

Cliff wasn't interested in a drink - just answers.

Vi paused, she placed a comforting hand on top of his. "You know, the Plush Horse isn't just a gin joint? It's a *turn-key*."

"What exactly does that mean?" He knew, but he still had to ask.

Vi considered his honest, yet naive question for a moment before she answered him.   "Men and sometimes couples pay for a key." She thrust her chin to a fish bowl full of keys kept under guard by a robust woman. "Sadie and I work for Hazel, in the rooms those keys unlock."

Cliff's heart sank. His jaw locked as his stare turned cold.

She could see it on his face.

He took that drink - tipping it back.   The harshness of the booze burned going down, but he didn't care. Cliff looked Vi square in the eyes, "I want Sadie's key - how much?"

"Wow - you're *really* carrying a torch!" Vi looked the handsome Cliff over. "Sugar, it doesn't work like that." Her tone was soft almost empathetic.

"Then what do I have to do?"

Vi glanced over to Hazel.

Cliff followed her gaze.

"Sweet talk *might* help, but Hazel is all business. I suggest putting money where your mouth is."

Cliff stood with conviction and strolled over to meet the full figured woman guarding the keys.

Hazel's beady eyes took in the tall drink of a man coming her way. Her thin lips painted in a dark-raspberry Cupid's bow looked silly against her pale caked-face with two rosy rouge spots for cheeks.

Cliff collected himself before he spoke.

From across the room Vi watched in awe.

Hazel's large horse-tooth smile and sudden healthy glow told Vi he had her eating out of his hands. Soon she was fishing out a key from the fishbowl and graciously handed it over to Cliff. She tucked away a wad of bills in her over flowing bosom as he turned to walk away.

Vi shooed a couple of admirers away when Cliff returned to their table. "Are you goofy? That sure was a lot of cabbage!"

Cliff only cocked his head to her words, not really listening.

Cautiously, she asked, "Now what are you going to do?"

"I'll know when I do it." He said quietly.

The truth Vi revealed had somehow hurt Cliff. Worried for her friend, Vi reached out, laying a tender hand on his arm. "Just hear her out." Vi's amber eyes connected with Cliff's, "Please?"

*

Dejectedly inspecting the reflection staring back, Sadie brushed out her strawberry-colored hair. Her sad baby blues had no tears left to shed, except the feeling was still there.

Cliff's mind was racing. Confusion, frustration and anger surged as he climbed the stairs to Sadie's room. *What was he going to do?* He stood outside her door contemplating. He took a deep cleansing breath and blew it out hard before he knocked.

The knock on her door startled her. No one knocked. Setting the brush down on the vanity, she sighed and put her *working* face on before opening the door.

The shock of suddenly seeing Cliff standing before her took Sadie's breath away. Her knees wanted to buckle. It was all she could do to remain strong, conducting a business-like attitude as usual. Her voice a little shaky, "Won't you come in?"

Seeing her washed away all the turmoil he'd been feeling. Cliff couldn't be upset. He remembered the Sadie he'd met months ago in Chicago. She wasn't some common whore, there was more to her...much more. He saw her differently, and she deserved a chance. They deserved a chance.

She shut the door behind him, and then reached out for his hat. "Can I offer you a drink? I've got the good stuff, it's from Canada."

Handing her his fedora, he nodded to the drink offer. He couldn't believe she was here. He had been thinking of no one else but Sadie for months.

He was happy to have found her again; nevertheless seeing her here - hurt. Until this moment, Cliff hadn't realized the genuine feelings he had for this woman. Knowing that she was a woman of ill repute was quite a shock.

Sadie's back was to Cliff. Dropping a few cubes of ice into each rock glass, she poured whiskey two-fingers deep, one for him and one for her. She had always hoped she'd see him again, but not like this; not ever like this. She never wanted him to know what she did.

Turning to face Cliff she caught the disappointment on his face. Her brilliant blue eyes met his as she handed Cliff his whiskey. For a moment her heart stopped. Sadie needed to turn away from this hold he had on her.

The room filled with uncertainty, as tension filled the space between them.

Nervously tapping her blood-red lacquered nails to the glass, Sadie took a breath, pausing as she looked down into her whiskey. *Another time, another place, maybe they could be, but here in the real world there's no way a girl from the wrong-side of the tracks could ever be with a well bred man.*

She crossed his path to sit seductively on the bed. She got used to taking off her clothes, but didn't want him to mistake her comfort for casualness. Her silky robe fell open revealing the top of her stockings. She took a steep drink.

Cliff couldn't look away from Sadie's shapely legs. Just being in her presence made him tremble a little inside. He stood uncomfortably silent for a long moment, just gazing at the beautiful woman he remembered from that night in Chicago.

Through the long silence and tension-filled air Sadie managed to ask, "Are we going to do this or not?"

Her words bit into Cliff. It took him back a little. Although her words upset him, he understood the coolness in them. This isn't what either one of them wanted. He looked at her for a long moment. Looking down into his glass as he tipped the ice cubes side to side before taking a drink. He looked back at her, into those beautiful blue eyes that filled his dreams.

Sadly he said, "I'm afraid not."

To her surprise his words cut her to the quick. Hurt, she quickly glanced away.

"But...if you'd permit me, I'd like to court you, Miss Sadie?"

She started to laugh, and turned her gaze back to Cliff. "Are you daft? You don't know what you're saying!"

"It sounds crazy, I know, but since that night I met you in Chicago, I have thought of no-one else. Sadie, I am not a naive man. I know what you do here behind closed doors."

"Oh that's rich! You *want* to date a whore?"

"I fell for that gal I met in Chicago. I want to know *you*, Sadie. I want to be with *you*."

Her hands started to shake, making the ice in her glass rattle.

Cliff took the drink from her hands, setting both of their drinks on the nightstand beside the bed.

She was confused. The shield she kept up to protect herself from getting hurt was weakening.

He took a knee, taking her hands in his.

They looked longingly into each other's eyes.

Averting his glance, a painful knot lodged itself in Sadie's chest making it difficult for her to breathe.

He looked around her small room. "I don't care about this, Sadie."

Stunned by his words, she quickly looked back to him. Not by any wild imagination could she believe this was happening.

"Sadie, I only care about the woman you are and how I feel about you."

"You don't know what you're saying!"

"Yes - I do! This? *This* is just a job. *This* doesn't define *you*."

For the first time in years, Sadie's eyes began to water. She thought she had control of her feelings. She detested being vulnerable. "We had one night! You don't know anything about me!"

"I know enough. I know I want to be with you, Sadie. But - I want to do this right. If you'll have me, that is?"

Feeling over-whelmed, her tears just kept coming. How she wanted to turn them off. She felt weak. She hated to feel weak. This man stirred wild thoughts and desires in her. She always dreamed of normal. She wanted that once-in-a-lifetime happiness. All little girls want the fairy tale. This can't be really happening. Not to her.

Sadie chewed her bottom lip; if she were to ever take a chance now was the time.

"Sadie, I know you think this is insane. Maybe I am? But - I know I want to take this chance with you. I'm hoping you do too."

She nodded *yes*.

He wrapped his arms around her and held her tight.

February 25th 1928

"Tonight, the gin-joint was full of bimbos and the lobby of the Plush Horse turned into another petting party. My dogs were tired and I retreated to room-4. My turn-key was a man named Cliff. He's no cake eater; he's sweet. He walked back into my life and wants to take me away from all of this. What do I do? Things still look dark, and I pray for strength. I'd love to start my life over. I hope he was real, because right now I think I'm dreaming."

Chapter 8

Cliff needed to wrap his head around what he was about to do. Jon was his best friend. Seeking guidance from his mentor, Cliff met him for breakfast at the Badger Hotel.

"What's got you so wound up?"

"Sadie is here in Burlington."

"That's great - so what's the problem? Is she married?"

"I found out she and Vi work at the Plush Horse."

Jon laughed. "Your moll is a pro skirt? I didn't see that comin'!"

Cliff was silent. Ignoring Jon's crudeness, he took a sip of coffee and set the cup back on the saucer. He tapped his thumb to the rim of the cup before looking up to meet Jon's eyes. In a low unwavering tone he said, "Jonathan, I respect you, which is why I've asked you here this morning. I have thought of no one else since I met Sadie in Chicago. That woman is special. She isn't just some skirt. Even when I saw the truth of what she did staring me right in the face, Jon, damn me to hell, I didn't care. I want to be with that woman. Tell me if I'm making a big mistake?"

Jon considered Cliff's words. "You're dizzy with that dame!"

Cliff blankly stared at Jon from across the table.

"I don't know why it matters what I or anyone else thinks. You're not asking for my permission, so what are you asking?"

"I don't know. This is huge. I may be making a terrible mistake for Sadie and for myself."

"What the hell do I know? I loved one woman in my life, and she left me all too soon. In the beginning it wasn't easy. Her father didn't much care for me. You see, he put value on a man's worth by the calluses on his hands." Holding out both of his hands to show Cliff, "Do you see any calluses on these hands? I went to college, earned my degrees and use my brain to make people's lives better. My wife loved me and supported my work until the day she died. But don't get me wrong, it was very hard on her. She missed her family and it saddened her that her father would never come to terms with her decision to be with a scientist. We all make choices in life, right or wrong, that's for ourselves to decide. If you want to try to make things work with Sadie, then do so whole heartedly."

*

Privately negotiating the terms of Sadie's termination from servitude wasn't an easy task. Cliff more than compensated the woman for her loss of income. Though Cliff would never tell Sadie he bought her freedom. She'd been through so much in her life, protecting her from certain truths was the least he could do to help her move forward.

To celebrate Sadie's fresh start, Cliff wanted to treat her to a special day. All women appreciate a day that's all about them. First he'd take her to buy a new dress.

On this particular sunny Saturday afternoon, it was nice enough to stroll through the shops. The streets were clear and the light dusting of snow had melted off the sidewalks. Walking hand in hand, they got a few inquiring looks. Most people paid no attention; however, those inside the dress shops were another story.

March 3, 1928

Cliff took me dress shopping today. I was really uncomfortable with the way the ladies in town were looking at me. Their gossiping tongues were wicked.

He saw how reluctant I was to even look at the dresses. Cliff must have sensed why and escorted me out of that one only to take me to another shop. This time Cliff took me by surprise. He had this polite yet commanding voice that got the owner of the shop to personally take care of me. She showed me some lovely frocks and even fitted me.

Cliff picked out a gorgeous navy blue wool-crepe dress for me. It fit me like a glove. I could tell it was pricey. The look the woman gave Cliff told me so, but he didn't even flinch. He just added a pair of matching shoes and a lovely hat to go with it. I couldn't believe it. We left with three outfits!

I happily carried the hatbox while Cliff walked me back carrying the packages. To my surprise, he told me he was picking me up at 8 in the morning for church. He kissed me on the cheek and left.

He is the sweetest man. But I don't know about going to church!

March 4, 1928

I was so nervous. I hadn't been to church since Mama died. I didn't feel worthy; I was scared.

Cliff looked so handsome in his dark gray Brooks Brother's suit. I wore the navy blue dress he picked out.

He took me by the shoulders and looked me in the eyes. "I'll be with you the whole way."

That man gave me strength. He gave me the courage to walk into that church.

Cliff held my trembling hand. Hushed whispers spread throughout the congregation as we walked in to find a seat. One woman gave us the stink-eye. Another looked down her nose at me. Some of the men had that flash of recognition, and if their wives caught them, they got an elbow. All the pews seemed full. The closer to the pulpit we got no one had bothered to offer a seat.

I kept my head held high, but was secretly dying from embarrassment inside. Halfway down an older woman politely smiled and moved in for us to take seats next to her in the pew.

I felt gossiping eyes glaring at me. It was positively scandalous - having a whore in church.

Cliff never wavered. He held my hand tightly. I'll never forget the look he gave me; the pride to have me by his side. This crazy fool really does love me.

The woman sitting to my right was very kind. She didn't seem at all concerned to be sitting next to the whore in church.

She had a warm smile and kindly blue eyes. "Welcome my Dear - I'm Lavern."

I was taken by her kindness and non-judgmental approach. I shyly returned the smile. "It's a pleasure to make your acquaintance. I'm Sadie, and this is Cliff."

Cliff politely shook her hand.

The organist pounded out a hymn. After that the service dragged on. I had forgotten how long church services were and how uncomfortable the hard wooden pews were. But somehow, I felt lighter that day. Everything seemed to be so difficult for me, yet I survived.

After church, we got to talking to Miss Lavern. Come to find out she was a widowed woman, who lost her soul mate, the love of her life in The Great War. She was a schoolmarm who ran the boarding house for women just north of Commerce Street.

Her hair, now graying, but her blue eyes still sparked with a passion for life. She may have been little but a mighty woman, who dared to break rules with God on her side; right was right. She understood everyone had a past, what they did with their life's future is what counted.

Lavern surprised me when she invited me to move into her home.

March 6, 1928

My room is plain and simple, with white walls and trim. The curtains are trimmed with Battenberg lace. I like it. This is my fresh start.

I like Lavern very much. She makes me feel like I'm finally home. Today we went to the market, and I helped her prepare for supper.

Sadie wasn't a working girl anymore. She now had to find something to do to keep busy. Although Sadie's domestic skills were limited, she happily helped Lavern with the house and other chores. At the end of the day Lavern shared her bootleg wine with Sadie. They played cards for hours and just talked.

Lavern reminded Sadie of her own mother, and felt Lavern's genuine graciousness. Sadie was very grateful and wasn't about to let her down.

*

Sadie had been a bundle of bubbling nerves all day. She had never been on a real date before. After all, in her line of work there was never an opportunity for such things. She was pacing her bedroom floor, anxiously waiting for Cliff to arrive.

When he buzzed the front door, Sadie felt ill. Her stomach was all in knots. She took a few calming deep breaths, straightened her dress, and checked the mirror one more time before heading downstairs.

Miss Lavern had let him in. Cliff was such a dashing man; she tried not to feel so inferior to him.

His radiant smile made her weak in the knees. "Ready?" He offered his arm.

Sadie looked to Lavern, who gave her an encouraging smile and approving nod.

Returning a lovely smile to Cliff, she happily accepted his arm as he escorted her out. They walked a few blocks to the theater, and waited in a short line to buy tickets for *The Wind.*

Sadie really didn't care what movie they saw, she was just so enamored to be anywhere with Cliff.

Cliff held Sadie's soft delicate hand. Being so close to her raised his temperature a few degrees. Back at home being with beautiful women never affected him this way; however, now being here with Sadie, he was feeling all sorts of topsy-turvy. He couldn't take his eyes off of her; her beautiful smile, her twinkling blue eyes. He wanted to kiss her, and that wasn't the only thought on his mind. Cliff was used to women throwing themselves at him back home. They never meant anything because he knew they only wanted him for his family's money and status. Here, Cliff hid his true identity, from everyone. If he was going to find someone worthy they had to fall for him, not his money.

Cliff had fallen for this woman the first night they met. He wanted to do this right. She deserved respect.

After the movie, Cliff quietly walked Sadie home. Standing at her door he had felt the 'spark' between them. He hugged her good night. This time he wasn't as brazen as the first time he had kissed her. Cliff whispered in her ear, his lips brushed her earlobe, "I want to kiss you so badly right now."

The heat of his breath on her neck sent a thrilling tingle through her body. Sadie turned to face him. Her baby blues locked on his, "Then kiss me."

He hesitated. Cliff wanted to take things slow with her. He wanted to do this right, and he wouldn't taint their new relationship with tawdry lust, but couldn't resist tasting her sweet lips. His lips greeted her soft kiss; tender and so sweet.

Sadie wanted more. Just his mere touch stoked a fire that burned deep inside her soul. It was hard for her to damper these feelings, but she respected Cliff's wishes.

From that moment on, Cliff had dinner with Sadie and Lavern most nights. He was getting to know them both quite well.

He was grateful for the way Lavern took Sadie under her wing, and taught her many things, including how to cook. She was getting quiet good at it, too.

March 9, 1928

Cliff and I went on our first official date. When he came to the door I nearly panicked. I was so nervous, but I think he was, too.

When I saw him standing in the foyer making small talk with Lavern, my heart just raced. I can't believe we're really doing this!

Cliff's face just beamed when he saw me coming down the stairs.

He took me to see The Wind playing on the big screen. He held my hand the entire time, lightly stroking the back of my hand with his thumb. His touch thrilled me. I feel so comfortable with Cliff. He's sweet, and kind. How did I get so lucky to have a Dandy like Cliff falling for me?

Chapter 9

Lavern, dressed in her Sunday best, opened the door. She smiled brightly giving Cliff a warm welcome. "Sadie will be right down."

No matter how many Sundays Sadie attended Church; she still didn't feel comfortable going, although it did get easier.

The three walked to church, Lavern entered first followed by Sadie on Cliff's arm.

The whispers were no longer as obvious, however some of her past clients' wives continued to glare, making her feel unwelcome. Sadie had no intention of hiding. She held her head high and followed Lavern to their seats midway down.

After the service the priest shook hands at the door with his parishioners. Sadie usually slipped out unnoticed, but today the priest reached out for her hand on her way out.

A large lump lodged in Sadie's throat as he clasped her hand in both of his. She looked him in the eye anticipating something bad to happen.

"Happy Easter, Miss Nolan. God bless you, and thank you for coming!" The priest's words were honest and rang true.

Quite surprised by his words, Sadie bashfully smiled. Oddly enough it was his acceptance that boosted her confidence. She would return to church. She silently smiled, as she felt her mother's warm approval from heaven above.

After supper, Cliff and Sadie took up residence on the porch swing, sipping sweet-tea and watching the sunset. Keeping perfect rhythm with their gentle sway, they didn't need to speak much; just holding hands and stealing kisses.

Lavern saw the easy way they were with each other. Though she missed her husband terribly, seeing a newfound love between Cliff and Sadie pleased her. Lavern was happy for Sadie, and was hopeful this was a love that would grow stronger every day.

Sadie's kissable lips tasted of cherries and sweet-tea. Her bright blue eyes mesmerized him, and he just couldn't look away. She was a contradictory mix of sexy, sweet and young innocence. Sadie was a strong, smart, vibrant woman for her age. Her lovely angelic face was a beautiful mask to the cruelty she'd experienced. Cliff couldn't take that pain away, but he'd do what he could to change her destiny. He was smitten, and there wasn't anything he wouldn't do for her.

Sometimes Cliff had a hard time catching his breath, being so close to Sadie. No woman had ever made him feel the way she did. With the slight drop in temperature, Cliff placed his suit coat over Sadie's shoulders as she rested her head against his chest. Resting his cheek on her head, he noticed how her hair smelled of light fragrant roses. He took-in everything about her.

Sadie took an interest in Cliff's work, although he didn't really talk about it, she wanted to know more.

"Tell me what you really do, Cliff. You said you're a scientist, but could you tell me what you do?"

Cliff pulled her in close. "I really can't talk about the project I'm working on. It's classified."

"Oh...okay."

Cliff could hear the disappointment in Sadie's voice. "I can tell you this though...we're on the verge of an incredible scientific breakthrough. Our DNA and genetics is all very new, and we're just beginning to understand it. We'll one day be able to correct weaknesses or even copy it!"

"That just sounds crazy. You're talking some kind of fiction."

Laughing, "That may sound like fiction now...but someday, it *will* happen. These are exciting times my, Love. You'll see."

"I have a feeling there isn't anything you can't achieve." Sadie proudly looked up into those incredible sexy brilliant eyes of his. Even his mind turned her on. She flashed Cliff a wickedly playful look.

Cliff leaned in to kiss her.

She greeted his tender kiss, but then nipped his lower lip with her teeth.

Sadie was something else. Cliff felt he just might have his hands full with this one, and loved every minute of it. "You little vixen, you! The things you do to me..." It was getting late and as much as he wanted to spend all night with her in his arms, he would do the right thing and leave at a respectable hour, keeping her honor.

Easter Sunday, April 8, 1928

Sunday morning Cliff arrived early to take Miss Lavern and me to Easter service.

Church service was good this morning. Cliff walked Lavern and me back to the house.

She had a roast in the oven for dinner. It filled the entire place with wonderful smells. He had brought wine to go with our meal and flowers for both Lavern and me. He is so thoughtful. Lavern just loves Cliff, and treats him as family.

After everything, I never dreamed of having such a meaningful relationship with such a wonderful man. I'm glad I took a chance with Cliff.

Chapter 10

April13, 1928

> *Cliff has been excitedly talking about the first Trans Atlantic flight between the U.S. and Europe. He told me one day he'd take me to Paris or anywhere in the World I wanted to go. He said we would fly there. Can you imagine such a thing? Flying to places I've only read about? I love Cliff's adventurous side. He's so full of life and wild ideas.*

Cliff adored Sadie. She still had no idea the life Cliff could offer her. Many times he thought about telling her who he was, who his family was. Sadie would never have to worry about anything.

The prospect of taking her on a World-wide adventure was such a thrilling plan. One he'd make sure to execute as soon as his contract had been filled with the War Department.

The weather was warming. Cliff enjoyed the smell of spring in the air. Working long hours in the sublevels of the secret labyrinth was taxing. Just the mere thought of Sadie gave Cliff a brief escape during the workday.

This morning, Nebraska opened the door for Cliff, greeting him with his usual friendly smile as he entered. "Mornin', Mr. Cliff!"

"Good morning to you, too, Nebraska! How are things?"

"Oh, things is good, real good, Mr. Cliff," Giving Cliff a large happy grin. "Thanks for asking."

"Glad to hear it." Cliff politely smiled back at his friend.

"Oh, Mr. Cliff?"

"Yes?"

"Thought you's might want to know, you's got guests this mornin'."

"Do I now?"

"Yes, Sir, Mr. Cliff. That Mr. Nickel's fella, and another gentleman."

"Thank you, Nebraska." Cliff returned the smile to his new friend, and cautiously headed down.

The brunette, more stoic than usual, was sitting behind her desk totally ignoring him as the armed guard checked his credentials before allowing him access.

Dr. Clifford Westbrook and Dr. Jonathan Blake had been working there for months. Getting checked in every morning, and having their cases checked every evening. It had become such a redundant routine.

The irritated Dr. Blake immersed himself with his work, in an attempt to avoid Mr. Nickels, who was waiting in their office with the other man.

Untrusting of the man, Cliff remained guarded but professional. "What can I do for you this morning, Mr. Nickels?"

"Dr. Westbrook, I want you to meet Dr. Albert Schmidt. He'll be your new assistant."

Not wanting to be completely rude, Cliff shook the man's hand. Albert appeared quite stiff with his high forehead, brooding brow and stern features. The dark circles under his intelligent blue eyes made him look older than he was.

"Dr. Schmidt, I need to have a word with Dr. Westbrook. Why don't you go ahead to your new station, I'll catch up with you." Nickels instructed.

Albert was all business as he quietly nodded, and exited.

Cliff turned to Nickels, "Excuse me, Sir, but I'm a bit confused. We didn't request an assistant."

"No; however, we feel he will help you speed things along."

"The Science cannot be rushed."

"Dr. Westbrook, we have been more than patient. We've allowed you access to confidential material. We have changed the course of our research, and we now need to see some sort of progress for our efforts."

Cliff narrowed his eyes, "What is it *exactly,* the War Department wants from us?"

"The War Department has put its top scientists together. The three of you should be able to create a better serum than the ones before you."

With a bitter taste in his mouth, Cliff spat out his thoughts. "The one's before us? More than half of their notes are blacked out! And whatever they did - they used those men down the hall as guinea pigs! The pain and sickness you've allowed them to suffer is unspeakable!"

"Dr. Westbrook - your moral, yet naïve outburst is admirable. As you so eminently pointed out, yes - we used human experimentation. It's a necessary evil, it may seem cruel to you; however, we are in a race, Dr. Westbrook. We don't have time to take the small careful steps you would suggest. We need an edge over our enemies. Killing them with poisons is easy and so common. I want to get more...creative!"

A chill surged through Cliff. He furrowed his brow, "Where does Albert fit in?"

"Albert will be helping you and Dr. Blake."

"You mean, he'll be watching us, and reporting back to you."

"If that's how you want to perceive this new addition to your team, so be it."

Agitated with their new situation, Cliff waited until Mr. Nickels had left the building before he joined Jonathan and Albert in the lab.

He curiously watched Dr. Schmidt interact with everyone in the lab. Wanting to know more about their new assistant, Cliff had to ask, "Tell me, Albert; what is your field of study?"

"Genetics."

Cliff and Jonathan shared a look. Until recently, agricultural genetics and bacterial genetics were iffy at best. However, mild breakthroughs have been quite successful. This left Cliff wondering what part Albert would play in all of this.

*

April 14, 1928

Cliff surprised me today. We took a walk downtown. Every time I'm with him I get nervous, a good kind of nervous. He excites me in a way I can't even begin to describe.

Cliff can be so spontaneous. He's fun, yet serious at the same time. We passed the Five & Dime and he got an impish look on his face before ducking in. They had an entire counter filled with glass jars of penny candy. Cliff got as excited as a child when he found the Salt water Taffy. Then he whimsically purchased a trinket bracelet, placing it on my wrist. I just love it! It's nothing special other than it's from him.

We left the Five & Dime holding hands, eating our candy, skipping and laughing like children. I didn't know I could be so happy.

Chapter 11

Cliff found the office void of his partner, and the coffee pot still held yesterday's cold coffee. Heading to the lab to find Jonathan, Cliff was distracted by strange noises chambering down the west tunnel.

He hadn't been down there since the day Mr. Nichols showed them the vault where they kept *test subjects.* Cautiously Cliff followed the cement tunnel, as he intently listened to the sounds.

With each step closer to the unsettling sounds, Cliff held controlled shallow breaths. Muffled as they were, a sudden painstaking cry stopped Cliff in his tracks. His heart pounded in his chest.

An armed guard seemed to appear out of nowhere, "Dr. Westbrook, can I help you with something?"

Working loose the lump that suddenly lodged in his throat; he managed to ask with some authority, "Who's working down here?"

The guard respectfully declined to answer, "I'm sorry, Dr. Westbrook; I'm going to have to ask you to turn back. If you want access, you'll have to get clearance through Mr. Nickels."

Cliff politely acknowledged the guard's position, with a nod, turned on his heels, and headed back to the lab to find Dr. Blake.

When he entered the lab the tension in the air was thick. Jon was silently angry about something.

"Where's our new assistant?"

Jon grumbled, "Don't give a damn as long as he stays out of my way!"

Cliff scanned the lab for Dr. Schmidt. He knew he wasn't in the office. His gut told him Schmidt had access to the test subjects that he and Jon did not. This realization bothered Cliff deeply. He would have to wait until after work to discuss his concerns with Jon.

It was Friday, yet felt like a Monday. Nothing was working right. The first two formulas somehow failed miserably. Everything was right, nevertheless they failed. Dr. Westbrook didn't want to believe their components were sabotaged. He just couldn't figure out any other logical reason for the failure.

Dr. Blake's radical approach bothered Cliff even if it made the most sense out of the past experiments. Based on his parting words with Mr. Nickels, this is what they wanted.

The problem was sustainability. Dr. Blake was just as frustrated as Dr. Westbrook.

Sometime after noon Dr. Schmidt appeared in the lab. Both Dr. Blake and Dr. Westbrook glanced up from their work in Schmidt's direction.

Albert ignored everyone's glances and proceeded to his workstation.

Cliff shared a silent look with his partner, then to Albert quietly working.

Neither one was happy with the stressful working conditions. It certainly wasn't conducive to their research. The free-thinking creative prowess of these two men had been hindered by Mr. Nickels and their new assistant.

*

Jonathan's family was always hospitable when Cliff joined them for dinner. His son remained just as distant as before, but his Granddaughter, Stella sure took quite an interest in her Grandfather and his work.

Stella had such a wonderful imagination. Jon enjoyed his time with her. "My goodness, Stella, what do we have here?"

Stella pulled her grandfather in close, with her hand cupped to her mouth and whispered in his ear. "I'm writing secrets."

Jon was quite impressed. "What kind of secrets?"

"Spy secrets!"

"But Stella, I don't see anything written?"

She put her finger up to her lips and whispered with enthusiasm, "That's because I'm using invisible ink!"

"Can you show me?"

Stella grinned from ear to ear. She loved her grandfather. In fact, she even thought maybe he was a spy and one day she could spy with him. She proudly took a large quill, dipped it in lemon juice and wrote a special message. Then she blew on it to dry it.

"Grandpa, could you light that candlestick for me?"

Jon lit the candlestick and handed it to Stella.

As Stella waved the parchment over the flame, Jon could make out the three words she wrote just for him. "I love you, too, dear Stella." He wrapped his arms around her in an embrace. "How did you become such a clever girl?"

Stella giggled and kissed him on his cheek. "I want to be just like you one day, Grandpa!"

Her mother called for Stella to go to bed.

"Good night, Stella, don't let the bed-bugs bite!" Jon watched Stella skip up to bed, before looking back down at her secret message to him.

Cliff offered Jon a drink. "She looks up to you."

With drink in hand, "I know she does. I've even caught her following me around town. She thinks she's being sneaky, but I know she's there." Jon smiled at the thought of Stella the 'super spy'.

"Jonathan, these are dark matters, and Mr. Nickels cannot be trusted. We need to be careful."

Jon motioned for Cliff to take a seat. "I agree. It was better with just the two of us. Now we have lab rats! Those sneaky bastards are reporting to Nickels for sure."

"We don't know what else they may be doing. I know that at least two different experiments have been tampered with." Frustrated, Jon let out a heavy sigh. "I can't get past the mess they created. It's crude; there's no finesse! I've tried to figure out their formulas but it's no use. They blocked out too much information!" He tossed an angry hand in the air. "We need to know more! If we could just break it down. I bet the poisons they created were harsh; in taste, color and weight. We need to take this in a new direction to be successful."

Cliff was shocked with Jon's words. "I've been thinking about the test-subjects. We need to get some samples from them. Albert has been telling me about his DNA and genetics research. Granted - it's in its infancy - but that got me thinking. I sure would like to see specifically, what the Fluorine toxins have done to these men. If it simply poisoned them or if it altered something?"

"Jon, those men are guarded, under lock and key. How do you propose we obtain samples from them?"

"We get permission from Mr. Nickels."

"Are you out of your cotton-picking mind?"

"You said it yourself, they are under guard. If Mr. Nickels wants a more 'creative' way to kill people, then he will grant us access to the test-subjects. He brought in Albert, so let's use Albert."

"You sound insane!"

"It's all relative ol' chap!"

"You *want* Mr. Nickels to think you have bats in the Belfry?"

Jonathan smiled wickedly, as he downed his drink.

Chapter 12

In Mr. Nickels earnest and greed to reach his objective, he handed Dr. Blake the key to the 'dungeon', just as he suspected. Now, gaining full access, Jon would oversee Albert and Cliff collecting samples from each test-subject. There was another area within the tunnels where the deceased were held. Most of the bodies had all ready been cremated. There were two, however, being held for disposal. Cliff carefully took extra samples from the deceased; of hair, bone, teeth and organs.

The scientists began to spend more time in the lab every day. They got to know each other and learn from one another. Neither Dr. Blake nor Dr. Westbrook trusted Dr. Schmidt. His wild ideas about altering human DNA to weaken and eventually kill off an entire populace, was outrageous. And yet that seemed to be exactly the direction their experiments were headed.

Today, Dr. Westbrook felt pretty positive about a solution, putting him in a good mood to start the day.

"Good morning, Nebraska!"

"'Mornin', Mr. Cliff!"

"Has Dr. Blake arrived yet?"

"Mr. Cliff, I's don't think Dr. Blake ever left last night. He's still down there."

Every day this week Dr. Blake stayed late and would be there when everyone else came. The frustrated Dr. Blake ignored everyone while he worked. Cliff was concerned, Jon was so lost in his work the world around him could collapse, and he wouldn't have noticed. Blake was even beginning to show signs of madness.

With coffee in hand, Cliff watched his partner work for a few minutes. "Good God, man - you stink!"

Cliff's comment broke Jon's concentration enough to look up at his partner.

With a devilish grin, Cliff offered a cup of steaming black coffee to his friend.

Jon accepted it with a grumpy frown upon his face.

"You slept here again, didn't you?"

Jon merely glared.

"I know you really get into your work, but you're starting to smell like the samples we took from the cadavers," Cliff said with a smirk.

Jon's glare darkened. "Cliff, quit being so sensitive."

Cliff took a sip of coffee. Laughing, "Okay, tell me what you're working on."

Bringing his hands together before him on the table, Jon started to share his ideas until Albert entered the lab putting a damper on their conversation.

Cliff thought about Jon's words and decided to take another approach. From what understanding he gained from Albert's explanation, Cliff realized the fluorine ion disrupted enzyme activity and attacked DNA and proteins.

By the end of the day Cliff found something. "Jon, take a look at this. When chemicals are dumped together, the elements that have a higher bonding affinity will 'steal' the bonds from other elements. Fluorine holds its electrons more tightly than any other element, and forms the smallest negatively charged ions of all the elements. This allows them to go where larger ions cannot. Therefore, fluorine ions can get into enzymes and DNA, and wreak biological havoc. Thus, damaging or destroying the original substance, disabling its biological radicals in the body, with its net electrical charge interfering with biochemical reactions!"

Dr. Blake took another look at what Westbrook was seeing.

"Jonathan, in each and every one of these men the concentration of Fluorine was too high. You are correct; they were literally poisoned to death and the others are on death's door."

"Then we need to find the correct percentage of Fluorine to use without the immediate death response."

Even Albert was surprised with Dr. Blake's frankness.

Dr. Blake was even more driven with finding a solution to Mr. Nickels' challenge.

Cliff swallowed his pride, getting his hands dirty working side-by-side with Albert. They ran tests on dead men's flesh, all along having a nagging feeling that Albert was working on another agenda; a secret agenda, one that only he and Mr. Nickel's were privy.

Upon leaving the 480 building, Nebraska grabbed the door for them. Cliff nodded to him, and this time Jonathan handed him a sawbuck.

"Thank you, Sir!" Nebraska said wearing a large smile.

They headed toward a local gin joint. Jon kept looking over his shoulder.

"Is there something wrong?"

"I'm not sure. I just have a feeling we're being watched."

"By whom? Not Albert or Mr. Nickels, so who would want to follow us?"

"I must sound paranoid?"

Cliff patted Jon on the back, and laughed, "A little bit, yeah."

Jon opened the door and took one last look back before entering.

That night, while Cliff helped Jon home in a drunken stooper, Jon mocked Prohibition. "Even the most pious drink wine!"

That gave Dr. Westbrook an idea. He knew the properties of Fluorine. If when mixed with other chemicals, the elements that have a higher bonding affinity 'steal' the bonds from other elements. Then Fluorine would be a perfect additive to wine. The trick was adding the right balance of Fluorine. This discovery would lead to a perfect way of distributing the serum created, but he had his reservations of what this could mean to the World.

Dr. Westbrook would work on this theory, but would only trust Jonathan with it.

*

Starting his day as usual, Cliff entered the 480 building eager to jump right into his work.

Nebraska greeted him, "G'Morning Mr. Cliff! Care for a shine?"

Curious, Cliff stopped in his tracks. Nebraska had never asked if he needed a shine before. Maybe he had something important to tell him. "Sure, why not." Cliff answered him, while climbing into a chair.

Nebraska got to work. Though he was a man of little words, this morning he was compelled to chat. "Your friend Dr. Blake came back late last night, and I don't think he's left. He had a strange look, too. I's gets the willies when somethin's off and I's got 'em. Just thought you should know, Mr. Cliff.

Cliff tossed Nebraska his coin and a little extra, as he nodded to him.

*

Dr. Blake approached his task as if looking for clues to solve a puzzle; each piece unique in itself. Jonathan noticed a common denominator amongst the files. Manipulating what he found was the challenge. When presented with a challenge, he would hit it head on.

"Good morning, Jon! Coffee?"

Blake didn't bother to acknowledge his partner. Reeking of corn whiskey from the night before, he looked tired, but driven.

Cliff set the cup down, giving Jon space in which to work while going about his own design. Although Cliff had seen Dr. Blake like this before, even he was beginning to question Blake's sanity.

Blake fished his pocket book from his jacket. Folded in-between its pages was a note from little Stella. She scribbled a secret message that looked like an alien language for him to cipher. He smiled. This was the perfect time to take a break. Finding repeated symbols he tried a few different pattern codes. Then he remembered the cipher code she had used once before, using the line-shapes that surround each letter including a dot where needed. That first message asked him to read her a story. This one asked him to meet her at the soda fountain.

Jon chuckled to himself as he quietly got up, grabbed his hat, and left without another word to anyone.

Little Stella wore a Dandelion crown upon her head, patiently waiting for her grandfather at the counter of the drug store. She freely kicked her feet and joyfully hummed to herself.

Jon tapped Stella's right shoulder, only to come around to her left.

She turned quickly back to find her Grandpa standing there.

"May I?" Jon gestured to the seat next to her.

Stella giggled, enthusiastically nodding her head yes.

"So what shall we have today?"

Stella's eyes grew wide with excitement, "Let's share a banana split!"

15 cents later, a fantastic banana split covered with heaps of whipping cream, nuts and extra cherries on top was placed between them.

Jon always enjoyed their secret rendezvous. He smiled mischievously at the thought of giving Stella ice cream before her supper, and her disapproving parents.

Refreshed and back in the lab Jon opened his notes. Something was off. He realized someone had been looking through them. Luckily he kept key elements out. Jon glanced up and looked around the lab to the others working. None of them seemed to pay him any mind.

He looked back down into his notes, then back up from time to time. He couldn't prove it, but he knew his notes had been gone through. Except for Cliff, he was distrustful of everyone. From now on he'd be watching the rest of the staff more closely. He knew Cliff would call him paranoid. That was fine, he could live with that.

April 23, 1928

Today, I spent the day with Vi. Lord how I miss my friend. Just for fun we went bowling. It's Monday, so no one was there, really. But people still treat us different. Sometimes I can't tell if it's because we're whores, or because Viola is colored. No matter, we had a great day. We haven't had that much fun in a long time.

I told her all about Cliff. She told me she could tell how much in love I am with him. Vi is really happy for me. She also told me she was going to be singing for a private party at Deuces this Friday night. I'd love to go hear her sing, but it's a gentlemen's club only. Since I'm not a whore anymore, it's off limits.

Chapter 13

Things were different. Once again something had changed and Sadie took notice. Most nights, Cliff had dinner with Sadie and Lavern. Saturdays were their date night, and Sundays he took Sadie to church.

Their dinners had become less frequent. Saturday dates soon became every other, until he missed date night altogether. When he started to miss church, Sadie really worried.

April 28, 1928

I haven't see Cliff in over a week. I can't believe how I miss him. Lavern tells me I'm in love. She must be right, because he's all I think about. When we're together I can barely breathe, and I can't stand it when we're apart.

Cliff makes me feel wanted, and treats me like a lady. But there are times I feel he hasn't touched me because he's changed his mind about me. He deserves better than me. What could I possibly give him?

April 29, 1928

I'm worried. Cliff missed church this morning and our weekly dinner at Lavern's. Is it wrong of me to hope for something good for myself? I pray he's all right.

May 4, 1928

Cliff finally came over after work. He missed dinner, but Lavern insisted he eat something. After fixing him a plate she left us alone to talk. I think she knew how upset I've been.

He apologized for not calling on me. He told me things at work were getting complicated. Cliff's under a great deal of pressure, although he hasn't told me what he's working on, I can tell it's taking a lot out of him. He wants to make it up to me.

*

Jon spotted Cliff through the window at the Badger Hotel.

Cliff had just ordered a whiskey while he waited for Sadie in the dining room.

Jon checked out Cliff's suit, "Well aren't you spiffy?"

"Sadie's meeting me for dinner."

"May I? This will only take a moment."

Cliff motioned for Jon to take a seat. "Of course."

Jon signaled for a drink, and leaned in speaking cautiously, "I think that little Sap jumped the gun!"

Jon's words made Cliff uneasy. "What's going to happen when Mr. Nickels finds out it's not ready?"

"Well, it's a little too late for what ifs. I've been watching men in black come in all day. I'm sure Mr. Nickels didn't invite them just to toot his own horn."

"You're sure they're government men?"

"I'm sure. Even the boys upstairs are nervous they're in town. They've closed the doors until these guys are gone."

Cliff looked down at the illegal drink in his hand, and took a sip anyway. "Any ideas on how we're going to keep the formula from getting into their hands?"

"I've already taken care of it!" Jon grinned, "It's child's play. Those geniuses will never figure it out." Taking a swig of his drink he diverted his attention to the stunning Sadie who appeared in the doorway.

Cliff turned to see Sadie scanning the room. Her navy dress of fine crepe hugged her soft curves. Her beautiful strawberry-hair was pulled back with a matching beaded headband.

When she spotted Cliff, her peachy face lit up full of joy. Her fluid entrance caught the attention of more than one man in the dining room.

"What a doll!" Jon stated what Cliff and the other men were thinking.

Cliff caught a glimpse of the mysterious spark Sadie held in those beautiful blue eyes. "You know I'm going to marry that girl one day!"

Both Cliff and Jon stood as she arrived at their table. Cliff pulled out the chair for Sadie.

She gracefully sat with her legs off to the side crossing her T-strap shoes at the ankle.

Jon excused himself, "Sadie". He bowed his head to her, and shook his partner's hand. "Cliff, you are *one* lucky son-of-a-bitch!"

"Have a good evening, Jon."

Cliff seated himself opposite her; reaching across their table he held her hands in his. His eyes locked intently on hers.

After long moments of silence, her cheeks began to blush. Just being near him made her quiver with excitement. This was new, different. This was love.

"My God, you are beautiful."

Sadie's cheeks darkened, "Cliff, people are beginning to stare."

"Let them stare. They're just jealous because I'm dining with the prettiest gal in town." He gave her a little wink, flashing his devilish grin.

Keeping in mind Jonathan's words, Cliff noticed a handful of men in dark colored suits entering the hotel throughout dinner.

Sadie noticed his distraction. "Is everything alright, Cliff?"

He brought his attention back to her. "Yes, of course."

Sadie looked past Cliff to the mirror behind him, "Who are those men you've been watching?"

Cliff smiled, surprised with her keen observance. "I don't know."

"You've been watching them all night. Are you sure everything is alright, Cliff, you seem distracted tonight?"

"Of course, my Dear," he lifted her hand to his lips, and kissed it. "There's nothing for you to worry about."

"That's what makes me worry!" Sadie leaned in and spoke softly, "You think they have something to do with what you're working on?"

Cliff couldn't keep much from Sadie. She was quite in tune with his thoughts. "Could be. Then again, it could be nothing. I rightly don't know."

May 7th 1928

Cliff told me not to worry. I'm not so sure. I've been watching the hotel fill up with men. They all seem to be waiting for something.

*

Jon left the Badger Hotel heading home; he felt the presence of someone watching him. He rounded the corner and spotted a suspicious dark sedan parked just up the street. Some men in dark suits approached him. The older, more seasoned man wearing a permanent scowl stepped up and flashed his tin, "Dr. Jonathan Blake? I'm Special Agent in Charge, Timothy Hughes."

Jon noticed this man wore the same silver signet ring as Mr. Nickels. He also had a Roscoe strapped under his arm, "Special Agent in charge of what?"

"I'm in charge of special projects, with the War Department. We need to speak with you."

Another non-descript man in black opened the back door to the sedan as Agent Hughes gestured for Jon to climb in.

Jon hesitated, he had a bad feeling about this, but curiosity won out, and he complied.

Agent Hughes followed into the back of the sedan with Jon, and the man who held the door closed it behind him.

"Dr. Blake, was that Dr. Westbrook sitting with you at the Badger Hotel?"

Not truly sure who these men were or what they wanted, Jon remained coy. "What's this all about?"

"Dr. Blake, when two of the nation's top scientists, in which we have a particular interest, disappear at the same time, we notice. When Germany's Dr. Albert Schmidt disappeared, there was a great concern, and we followed his trail here to Burlington. Low and behold, we find you and Dr. Westbrook in the same town."

"What are you talking about? We didn't disappear."

"Would you enlighten me as to why you three are here, in Burlington?"

"I can't do that. And *if* you really are who you say you are...then you already *know* that answer."

"Dr. Blake, I assure you I *should* know; however, whatever you think you're working on, it is *not* for the War Department."

Jonathan continued to be aloof. He considered Hughes words and wasn't sure what he should believe. Jon clammed up.

Agent Hughes was persistent, "Do you know a man named Jeremy Nickels?"

Although Jon contained a perfect poker-face, he was having some difficulty processing what Agent Hughes was suggesting.

Hughes carefully observed Jonathan's stoic presence. This lack of response puzzled him. "Okay, if you're not going to communicate with me, then just hear me out."

Jon gave Agent Hughes a subtle nod.

"I do not believe in coincidences, Dr. Blake. I do; however, believe you and Dr. Westbrook are working for Mr. Nickels under false pretenses. Whatever you are doing for Mr. Nickels, know that it is not supported by the War Department. We believe him to be a German sympathizer. We want Nickels, and you need to figure out whose side you are on before we take him."

This was far from what Jon expected.

A man in black opened Jon's door. He exited the back of the sedan stepping out into the street. Agent Hughes' men climbed in, and Jon watched as they drove away.

Cliff's words rang true, these *were* dark times. If Jon was unsure of Mr. Nickels before, this new information gave Jon the confirmation he and Cliff suspected; however, he didn't feel Agent Hughes was to be trusted either.

*

Cliff was surprised to find Jonathan waiting outside his door first thing in the morning. "Jon?"

"I think we better step back inside."

Holding the door for Jon, Cliff asked, "What's happened?"

"I had an interesting encounter last night after I left the Badger Hotel."

"Do tell."

"A man, Special Agent Timothy Hughes approached me last night and insisted I get into the back of his sedan. Long story short - he told me Mr. Jeremy Nickels isn't with the War Department."

"What?"

"He also said that you and I had disappeared and he was surprised to find us here in Burlington, Wisconsin with Dr. Schmidt."

"What in the hell are you talking about, Jonathan?"

"I really don't understand it myself. I don't know who to believe. This Agent Hughes said that whatever we think we're doing for the War Department, its unofficial and off the books. He's even looking for Mr. Nickels. Apparently the War Department wants him. What does *that* tell you?"

Cliff sunk down into a chair. An uneasiness filled him. "That tells me we can only trust ourselves." He looked up to the agitated Jonathan. "We cannot let on that we know any of this."

"Hughes wants to meet with us. I don't trust these government men. They're slick - too slick. I'd much rather work with the outfit. At least you know what's what!"

Chapter 14

June 2, 1928

Cliff had something special planned for Sadie's birthday. He sent Nebraska to the boarding house to deliver part of his surprise.

Lavern made her way to the back door. "Nebraska? It's a bit early, don't you think?"

"Yes, Ma'am...Mr. Cliff sent me over with these packages and a letter for Miss Sadie."

"Oh, well, don't just stand there...come on in. I'll fetch her."

Sadie excitedly bound down the stairs and ran to meet Nebraska.

"Woah - Miss Sadie, you's might want to slow down." Nebraska chuckled.

"Are those for me?"

Chuckling at her overly zealous outburst, "Yes, Miss Sadie. They's from Mr. Cliff." Fishing a letter from his shirt pocket, "This is for you, too."

Quickly snatching the letter from Nebraska, she read it first to herself, and then aloud.

Happy Birthday, Sadie

If you'll do me the honor of joining me this evening, I have something very special planned. I hope I guessed correctly. I shall pick you up at 7 o'clock. I look forward to seeing you in these. With all my love, ~Cliff

"Can you believe it?" Sadie squealed, grabbed her packages and ran back up to her room.

Lavern and Nebraska stood in the kitchen just looking at each other, amazed at Sadie's reaction, gradually working their way to lightly chuckle.

"Well, Nebraska, care to join me for a cup of coffee?"

"Yes, ma'am, a cup of coffee would be mighty nice." Nebraska happily accepted.

Lavern removed the piping hot pot from the stove top and poured a cup of coffee. Placing it on the kitchen table, "Come, and sit a spell."

"Thank you, Miss Lavern." He lightly blew the steam away. After taking a few sips, "Miss Lavern, this sure is some good coffee."

With a smile she replied, "It's the eggshells I mix in the grounds - they take the bitterness out of it."

*

Sadie painted her nails, by an open window to keep from getting dizzy from the fumes of her Revlon nail lacquer.

It seemed to take her all day just to get ready for this date. She and Lavern chatted like mother and daughter, and that seemed to help the anxiousness Sadie felt.

The dress fit her perfectly. Cliff had splendid taste in fine clothes; everything came from the House of Chanel.

Cliff's car could be heard pulling up to the house. The time had come for her very special date. Lavern let him in, greeting him with an approving smile. "She'll be right down." Lavern placed a caring hand on cliff's arm, as she leaned in and spoke softly. "She's a bit nervous."

At the top of the stairs Sadie stood poised. Her makeup was little to nil, showing off her fresh peachy skin. She wore the little black silk, Chanel dress Cliff sent her. Even the shoes fit her perfectly. Her gloved hands clutched a small beaded handbag.

Cliff was mesmerized by the presence of her subtle beauty. Sadie was eloquent and womanly.

Lavern smiled with shear pride as they left.

They drove out to the Aquilla Resort Pavilion for dinner and dancing. The place was huge. Its parking lot was lined with fancy cars. Some of them had drivers that stayed with their cars. The doormen wore tails and white gloves.

Sadie felt like a princess, the way she was dressed and being catered to in such a fashion.

When Sadie removed her gloves, Cliff noticed she was wearing the little trinket bracelet he bought her at the Five & Dime. It made him smile. That's what he liked about Sadie. It wasn't about the gift, it was the gesture.

Cliff ordered a bottle of French Champagne for the table. The waiter poured a flute for Sadie and one for Cliff, and then replaced the bottle into the bucket beside them. Cliff raised his glass in a toast, "Here's to your 20th birthday, and may each one after be just as happy, and just as special as you are.

Sadie's face flushed pink. Her bright blue eyes watered with happiness as she took a sip of Champagne for the first time.

The bubbles tickled her nose.

Dinner was exquisite. As dessert came, Cliff placed a small rectangular box wrapped in gold paper and decorated with a matching ribbon on the table. It looked expensive. Sadie looked to Cliff with a happy surprise in her eyes. "What's this?"

"It's your birthday present, silly girl."

It had been years since she'd received a birthday gift. Sadie pulled the tie of the bow and then carefully unwrapped the pretty paper. He had bought her perfume; Chanel No.5. "Oh, Cliff, you shouldn't have! This is all too much."

The look on her bright, joyous face told Cliff how surprised and happy she was. "I don't think so. Nothing but the best, for my gal."

The band in the ballroom played for hours. The singer wasn't Viola, but she was good. Cliff and Sadie danced the night away.

This man saw Sadie; really saw Sadie. That night in Chicago she had stolen his heart. There would never be another woman for Cliff.

*

July 4, 1928

Another perfect day! Cliff took me down to the parade, followed by a carnival in Echo Park. Lavern helped me pack for a picnic lunch, complete with dessert! I hadn't baked a cake since Mama was alive, but Lavern helped me with that, too. The best pineapple upside-down cake Cliff has ever had! So he says.

Once again, we received curious glances. I felt it, but Cliff said he didn't care what anyone else thought about us. I tried my best to ignore the small-town, small-minded stares. It's amazing how all my insecurities vanished with just the touch of his hand. I don't know how he does it, but nothing else matters when we're together. He makes me feel like I'm the center of his Universe.

We went for a walk along the lake. Cliff took off his socks and shoes, and rolled up the legs of his trousers. I slipped off my sandals so I could feel the sand beneath my feet. We laughed and talked until the fireworks started.

Finding an opportunity to slip away from the crowd, we revisited a secluded spot we'd found earlier in the day. It was a lovely romantic spot. I couldn't keep my hands off him. We shed our clothes to take a swim. After our risky swim, he laid out the blanket from our picnic on the beach. His hungry kisses ignited my burning desire for him. I felt his passion brewing deep inside him. I embraced the pleasures of his every touch. There was such electricity between us. I'd never had that. This was new for me. He told me how happy I made him! I am surely smitten.

Cliff laid me down and held me close. He smelled wonderful. A good manly scent. His lips tasted mine, and his wonderful hands explored my curves. How he made me feel, I have never thought love could be like this. He quietly sought permission to mount me. I easily gave into him with titillating responses. He was so gentle, and loving, yet it was so intense. I have never enjoyed the touch of a man as I did today, with Cliff. I now know what making love is. Tonight, under the fireworks we made love for the first time, and I know our lives were changed forever.

Chapter 15

Finding Nebraska's chair vacant, Cliff stopped to have his shoes shined before heading out. As always, Nebraska smiled warmly and got to work.

"How's business?"

"Business is good, real good - Mr. Cliff."

"And you're other business?"

Nebraska gave Cliff a sly smile. "Oh - I's ready to retire from that one, Mr. Cliff." He finished shining Cliff's handcrafted leather shoes.

Admiring the perfect shine Nebraska gave his shoes, "You sure do one heck of a job, Nebraska! Here, this is for you." Cliff handed him a bill along with a message for Nebraska to meet him and Jon later that night.

*

Jon met Cliff at the train station precisely at 10:00 p.m. "What the hell is this all about, Cliff?"

"Did anyone follow you?"

"No, I left through the back way of the gin joint just like you asked me to."

Cliff led Jon into the grainery and down some concrete steps to the subbasement. He knocked on the door with three rapid sessions.

Nebraska opened the door and let the two in.

Jon looked around, "Why are we meeting here?"

Nebraska stood by quietly.

Pointing in Nebraska's direction, Cliff answered, "He has the key to our dilemma."

Jon raised a curious brow, and looked at the shoeshine man, "What would that be?"

"The wine, Jonathan. Fusing the formula with the wine."

Jon glared at Cliff while he processed the idea.

"Jon, you said it yourself, 'Even the most pious drink wine.'"

"Well I'll be a son-of-a-bitch. We *could* ferment the formula with the grapes, but we'll need to watch it closely. We need to be in full control of the entire process to work."

"That's why I just bought Nebraska's operation here."

"You did what?"

"I just bought everything we need to do this. All we need to do is bring all this into the lab, via the tunnels, of course!"

"I think my insanity has rubbed off on you." Jon smiled, "Well, what are we waiting for?"

The three men moved the contents of Nebraska's winery to the lab. They saved the vat for last.

Rigging a skid with cart wheels they carefully rested the vat on its side and tied it down. Cliff and Nebraska pushed while Jon pulled the contraption down the tunnel.

Jon started to express amusement. To himself at first, but then it morphed into a full bellied devilish laugh.

In a relatively hushed tone, Cliff snapped. "What is wrong with you? Be quiet, Jon!"

Both Cliff and Nebraska shared a bewildered look as they patiently waited for Jon to gather himself, before they continued.

The trick was getting it through the iron gate. Nebraska chiseled the brick away from the bolts to remove the gate. After they had moved the vat into the lab and set it up, they returned to re-brick and set the gate in place. The mortar would still be wet but they didn't figure anyone would notice.

"Thank you, my friend. Without you, we couldn't have pulled this off."

With a mischievous twinkle in his eye, Jon shook Nebraska's hand, "Yes, thank you, man."

It was obvious that Dr. Blake eagerly wanted to get started.

The men trekked back through the iron gate, and down through the tunnel to the subbasement of the grainery.

"Now you's need to leave here first. I'll wait a bit before I's go. Make sure you's not seen."

Dr. Blake had been deep in thought. Obviously already working out their theory in his head, and how they were going to procede. Cliff placed a reassuring hand on Nebraska's shoulder, "Your secret is safe with us."

*

Cliff and Jon arrived together at the lab early. Just like they had hoped, they were the first ones there. The mash was set-up last night. The garbage can was filled with dark purple stained cheesecloth, next to Jon who jotted a few notes down in his pocket book.

They were in full swing of their work by the time others straggled in, and they received some pretty curious looks.

Albert came in and froze. He couldn't figure out how or why all this equipment was here. This frustrated the man. "What are you doing?" He barked. "What is all this?"

Jon merely glanced up to acknowledge Albert's outburst.

"I demand to know what is happening here!"

"If you must know, we're making wine, genius!"

The vein on Albert's forehead pulsed. "This is a science lab! Not a distillery!" Albert yelled. His German accent slipped through in his anger.

Jon stopped what he was doing. He looked at the red-faced man. "Easy, Fritz! We're conducting a scientific experiment, a delectable one, but an experiment non-the-less."

The entire lab quieted. They stopped what they were doing to watch the battle of wits ensue.

"What in the hell is the matter with you? Dr. Blake, you must know this is a bad idea. We work for a government agency and need to respect the prohibition laws. You can't make bootleg wine in this facility!"

Jon shared a look with Cliff before taunting Albert further. Jon shrugged his shoulders, "You see we have everything already set up and working. Subsequently, we will ruin this batch if we disrupt it! We will continue with our experiment, thank you."

"Do not dismiss me! Do you think this is a game?"

In a superior yet dissonant tone, Jon fired back, "Listen, Fritz, this isn't a game. I told you - this is an experiment. I do not need to seek your approval nor include you in my theories. Obviously you have a problem with the way I work. Maybe you should take the day off, and think about your position here in this lab. If you still have a problem with it, I suggest you work it out with Mr. Nickels." Jon returned to his notes without another glance in Albert's direction.

Cliff along with everyone else watched as Albert turned and stormed out of the lab.

Two days later, Jon's paranoia set in when he discovered someone had been in his pocket book. He suspiciously watched everyone in the lab throughout the day. Albert was the only one who didn't pay him any mind.

Cliff caught the dark glare Jon gave Albert from across the room.

The course of power in the lab was in a constant struggle. They used Albert's expertise in genetics added to the sustainability Jonathan and Cliff needed.

Reluctantly they worked out the most devastating combinations with Albert; however, they didn't share their formulas with him. Instead, Jon had devised a cipher based on the codes he and his granddaughter Stella used to send each other messages. Cliff quickly adapted to using this same cipher.

The heated tensions in the lab kept Cliff on edge. He didn't want to expose Sadie to his troubles.

*

Lavern found Sadie sulking on the front porch swing. Covering Sadie's shoulders with a shawl she inquired, "A penny for your thoughts, my Dear?"

Sadie reluctantly replied, "Its Cliff."

"What about him?" Lavern asked as she sat down beside her.

"Lately he's been distant, and I haven't seen him in more than a week."

"Do you want my advice?"

Sadie's worried eyes desperately looked to Lavern and nodded her head, yes.

Placing a motherly hand on Sadie's, "Anyone can see how much he cares for you...but that man has something weighing on him. I think you need to let him work through whatever it is and just be here for him."

Lavern was right, but Sadie missed Cliff terribly. She needed to see him.

Sadie packed a light basket of cheese, fruit and bootleg wine. Wearing a flirtatious sundress and her hair tied up with a ribbon, leaving little tendrils of loose strawberry-hair falling on her bare shoulders, she knocked on Cliff's hotel room door unannounced.

Cliff slowly answered the door, unshaven, and looking drained. His white sleeveless T-shirt and dress trousers looked like he'd slept in them. Distracted, he happily sighed and let her enter.

His bare feet padded across the wooden floors. He cleared the table and a chair for her to sit.

Sadie took in his room, which was in slight disarray. The Emerson table fan made a soft steady hum as its 3-brass blades oscillated.

"When was the last time you ate?"

Cliff cocked his head, "What day is it?"

"It's Saturday."

"I think Thursday."

Sadie didn't scold; she just merely unpacked her basket. Slicing off pieces of cheese and offered him a cluster of grapes.

Cliff opened the bottle of wine, and poured two glasses.

It tasted good going down. It was elegant, delicate, and full bodied. Cliff detected a hint of almond and its violet aroma. "Where did you get this?"

"It's delish, right?" Sadie said with an impish grin.

"Yes, yes it is. But where on Earth did you get this?"

"Nebraska made it."

Cliff smiled and took another sip. "He has talent, I'll give him that!"

After eating the treats from her basket in tentative silence, Sadie leaned in breaking their awkwardness. "Want to talk about it?"

Cliff's attentions were obviously elsewhere. He turned his dark tired eyes to Sadie. "I can't."

"Okay, then we won't talk about it. I don't know what's going on, but we need to clean you up. There is no reason to lose yourself."

"Now, where is your shaving kit?"

Cliff pointed in the general direction of his bathroom.

Sadie produced his shaving kit and a steaming towel. "Do you trust me?"

Intrigued, Cliff looked into her beautiful blue eyes and nodded - yes.

She wrapped Cliff's face with the hot towel.

He couldn't see what she was doing but heard her preparing the lather for his face. Then he heard her work the razor against the strap several times.

Sadie removed the towel and looked down at the trusting Cliff. "Ready?" Her sweet voice was soft yet confident.

She took the badger-hair brush full of shaving cream and worked it into a thick rich lather. Then she applied it to his face.

Leaning over him with the gentle brush of her bosom, Cliff lifted his face to her and found her lips; full, soft and so sweet. With that she took a swipe across his cheek with a very sharp straight razor.

His breath hitched with the first touch of the steel.

Sadie took another swipe across his cheek, slowly moving upward from his neck exposing his stubble free handsome face.

Her soft sent filled his lungs. With each slow even stroke with the sharp steel blade, Cliff's pulse quickened, his balls tightened as blood rushed to his aching groin.

She needed to get a better angle in which to shave his throat. Flashing Cliff a wicked smile, Sadie hiked up her skirt as she straddled his lap. Feeling his growing erection beneath her made her gasp, and she couldn't help but smile.

Trusting Sadie so completely with a sharp blade moving from his throat to his jaw, was the most invigorating sensation Cliff had ever felt. It really turned him on.

She lovingly wiped his face clean. "There, all done." Her mischievous blue eyes glistened.

Cliff passionately enfolded Sadie's body in his arms and kissed her. He kissed her hard on the mouth. She had aroused every cell in his body.

Not fully understanding the lapse in their relationship, Sadie understood this; his body language and hungry kisses. Sadie released his engorged sex.

His eyes connected to hers, as he let out a long breath.

The devilish look in her eyes told Cliff her intentions.

Cliff needed this more than he was willing to admit. Being inside Sadie, with her wrapped in his arms was ecstasy. Taking a firm hold of her Cliff stood from his chair, knocking it down. Sadie wrapped her legs around his waist as he securely carried her to the bed. He laid her down, all hands and hungry kisses; needing and wanting.

With her lips, she traced his freshly shaven jaw down to his neck. Her hot breath drove him crazy with desire. With her shapely legs wrapped around him, Sadie drew him deeper into her.

He could never have too much of Sadie.

Deep-rooted passion ignited between them. Their heated bodies responded with each touch.

Hearing her soft sighs of pleasure, Cliff released himself, filling her. Cliff savored the feel of Sadie's body against his. Softly stroking her strawberry-hair. Lying exhausted and happy in each other's arms, the sunlight moved across the room casting dark shadows in the corners as they talked, kissed and touched, getting to know each other intimately.

July 31, 1928

I'm glad I went to see Cliff. He has been working so hard. He is amazing in every way. Just being in his arms gives me the strength to change my stars. And when we make love, there isn't anything in this world better. I may be goofy, but I sure do love that man.

Chapter 16

August 20, 1928

The end of summer carnival was so much fun! Lavern even won 1st prize for her strawberry jam! That makes me feel good, especially since I helped her with it. Lavern has taught me a lot. I believe if my mother was still alive, she'd be much like Lavern.

Cliff won me a big teddy bear at the shooting gallery. I think he even surprised the carnie! I can't recall feeling so happy. My life sure has changed. I'm now surrounded by people who love me. Even Vi told me how proud she is of me.

August 28, 1928

Vi told me she was part of some deal Hazel made with the man who owned Deuces. Deuces' cliental weren't like the ones at the Plush Horse. They were known to be rougher. She's playing it cool, but how could she? She was forced into this. Vi is not property! I think I am more upset about it than she is. She's my dearest friend, and I want only the best for her.

Sadie met Vi at the speakeasy for a drink. They had so much to tell each other.

Vi had hardly recognized Sadie. She had transformed from the sweet lost little girl to a proper lady that carried herself well, wearing the confidence she'd gained over these past few months. "Let me take a look at you."

Sadie was bubbling over with joy.

"I take it things are going...well?"

Sadie was head-over-heels in love with Cliff. It was positively obvious.

Vi ordered a round of drinks.

Sharing most everything with her best friend that had happened since Cliff got her out of the Plush Horse. Vi was happy for Sadie. Very happy.

Vi then filled Sadie in on her new arrangement. She wasn't overly joyous about it, but it could always be worse.

Sadie barely touched her drink. It didn't taste right. Maybe it was a bad batch of booze.

Smoke swirled and danced around her head. The smell was making her nauseous. Sadie blew out a quick breath, but it didn't diminish the feeling of a warm damp blanket wrapped tightly around her. She felt the sudden urge to bolt from the bar, quickly making her way outside through the back door.

Vi followed her out.

Sadie bent over, inhaling deep cool breaths of fresh air, calming her nauseous stomach.

Vi reached out placing a delicate hand on Sadie's shoulder, "You okay, Chicky?"

Sadie's face was clammy and pale. Even her freckles had faded. Her blue eyes were watery. "Yeah, I think so. I just got over heated, I guess."

Vi, suspected something else entirely. "Come on, I'll walk you home."

August 29th 1928

I don't know what it is about Cliff. We have a strong connection. He trusts me, and has started to confide in me. Tonight Cliff told me he was a part of something that he cannot talk about.

August 31, 1928

I haven't been feeling well. Lavern just keeps smiling at me funny. She said she's going to have Doc. Newell come by.

September 1, 1928

I guess Miss Lavern knew what she's talking about. I'm pregnant! I can't be...when I was whoring I had always been careful. We were only together twice - how can this be? Lavern asked me when I was going to tell Cliff. Though I know he loves me, I'm worried - what will his reaction be? I am so scared to give to Cliff the news.

Lord - help me!

Sadie hadn't come down for supper. After the doctor left, Lavern was concerned with Sadie's reaction to the news. Climbing the stairs to Sadie's room with a tray Lavern could hear her sobbing behind her closed door. She lightly wrapped on the door, "May I come in?"

Through tears, "Mm-mm..."

Lavern set the tray with her dinner off to the side. She could only imagine what Sadie was feeling. It hurt to see her so torn. She sat on the bed next to Sadie, and put motherly arms around her. "Shhh, child. It'll be alright, now."

"I don't know how?"

"I know you're scared." She said in a tender voice. "You must know Cliff loves you. This child may be an unexpected surprise, but Sweetheart, a child is a gift from God. Embrace it."

"What if once he knows, he won't want me; or the baby?"

"I don't believe Clifford Westbrook is that kind of man. He is stronger than you know. I've seen the way he looks at you. That is love...pure love. And I know a thing or two about love."

Sadie buried her red, puffy, wet face into Lavern's shoulder. Lavern just held her, making her feel better about her condition; however Sadie was terrified to tell Cliff.

September 2, 1928

After church, Lavern gave us some space to work things out. She's great that way. She's so supportive and loving, like a mother to me.

I found the courage to tell Cliff my news. To my surprise he was happy, more than happy; he was excited. He really does love me. Why - I do not know, but I am truly blessed.

*

Cliff happily climbed into the shoeshine chair.

Nebraska quickly got to work.

"Nebraska, do you like shining shoes?"

"Yes, Sir, Mr. Cliff, it's a good job."

"You're a man of many talents, Nebraska. A man who could change his destiny."

Nebraska continued buffing Cliff's left shoe didn't bother to look up, "Is that so, Mr. Cliff?"

"If you're that man, I've got a proposition for you."

"What kind of proposition would that be, Mr. Cliff?" Nebraska asked as he started to polish Cliff's right shoe.

"Well Nebraska, I find myself in need of an associate, and I believe you'd be a perfect fit for the job."

Nebraska finally looked up, "Associate? What exactly would your *associate* be doin', Mr. Cliff?"

"That depends on how well you like shining shoes." Cliff smiled, looked around the lobby, and then back to Nebraska. "I need an associate to be my eyes and ears. I'd also like him to run errands for me and Miss Sadie if need be. He'd be paid every Friday, whether I have something for him that week or not."

"Mr. Cliff, that's a mighty nice offer, but my Mama always said, if it sounds too good to be true, it probably is."

"Your Mama was a smart woman."

"I's likes you Mr. Cliff. I can tell you're not like these other fellas comin' and goin' out of this place. Why don't you's tell me more about this associate position?"

Cliff chuckled, "Alright Nebraska, how about you have lunch with me today? We'll discuss it then."

"You know, a colored man's got no business being in here if he wasn't shining shoes. It'd be a good thing for me to keep on doin' if you's wants me to be your eyes and ears."

Cliff stood, admiring the wonderful job Nebraska did on his shoes. He paid the man and then some. "Smart and talented; I knew I found the perfect man for the job."

Right at noon, Nebraska came calling, knocking on the back door of Miss Lavern's boarding house. Lavern had prepared a fried chicken lunch that Nebraska could smell from the street.

"Come on in, Nebraska, Cliff is waiting for you in the kitchen." Lavern was polite and took Nebraska's hat.

Corn on the cob, coleslaw, potato salad and a platter full of country fried chicken filled the kitchen table. It all made Nebraska's mouth water.

"Please, take a seat, join us for lunch." Cliff offered, "Sweet-tea?"

Nebraska anxiously looked around the large room; Sadie warmly greeted him with a smile as Lavern grabbed an extra glass of sweet-tea for him. Taking the chair across from Cliff, Nebraska sat down nervously.

Neither Cliff, Sadie nor Lavern had a problem with Nebraska sharing a meal at their table. However; this was all very new for Nebraska, he had never eaten with white folks before. He enjoyed their easy ways, and friendly conversation.

After their meal, Sadie helped Lavern clear the table and set out the peach cobbler for dessert, while Cliff spoke more about the position he offered Nebraska earlier in the day.

"Do you have a Sunday suit, Nebraska?"

"I do - it's old, but Jesus don't mind."

Cliff smiled. He enjoyed Nebraska's honest quick wit. "Well, I'd like to buy you a new suit for your new position."

Nebraska stared at Cliff blankly.

Cliff looked down at Nebraska's worn brown boots. "What size shoe do you wear, Nebraska?"

"Well, Mr. Cliff, if I's buying 'em - I's wear a 10 1/2, but if you's a given 'em to me - I's wears anything from a 9 to a 12."

Cliff chuckled, "Okay, Nebraska. Let's go buy you a new suit and pair of shoes, size 10 1/2."

"Mr. Cliff, why me?"

Cliff considered Nebraska's question for a moment. "Nebraska, *you* are a smart guy, you are my friend. I trust you. I only want good things for you."

Nebraska looked down to his hands folded on the table, and then back up to Cliff's sincere gaze. "I'll do my very best for you, Mr. Cliff."

Cliff offered his right hand, "Welcome aboard, Nebraska."

Nebraska accepted Cliff's hand, and shook it. "Thank you." All of this was strange and uncertain. Nebraska never felt he could drop his guard, but Cliff was different. He was a straight shooter and an honorable man. Nebraska had great respect for Cliff.

Chapter 17

Walking home from the butcher shop with Lavern, Sadie spotted Cliff and Jon speaking with three men in black suits one block up. Cliff seemed ridged, and the look on his face was stern.

Sadie was curious as to who the men were, talking to Cliff, but kept her head down and walked on by. She had many questions about what Cliff really did. Seeing him looking so angry bothered her.

Lavern picked up on Sadie's troubled thoughts. "Don't fret, my Dear; their work is a delicate mistress."

September 17, 1928

Lavern and I spent the day taking out some of my dresses. They've gotten a bit tighter these days. Cliff has been more secretive than usual. I have a bad feeling about it, but Lavern assures me I can trust in Cliff.

Sadie wanted to surprise Cliff. The look on Cliff's face yesterday had been eating at her. She understood there were things he couldn't tell her, but Sadie thought she could at least release some of that tension he'd been carrying around.

Coming in through the back door to the hotel and making her way up to Cliff's room, Sadie was becoming more excited with what she was about to do.

She lightly knocked on Cliff's door. There was no answer. Not wanting to be too discouraged, she knocked a bit harder. Still no answer!

Sadie turned to leave and was approached by a sinister looking man in black coming up the hall. The lights in the hall brought attention to the silver signet ring he wore.

"Miss Nolan?"

Surprised this man knew her name; she stopped and turned back to him. "Yes?"

"I see we're both looking for Dr. Westbrook."

Sadie didn't answer right away. She paused, looked this man in the eye, and said, "Pardon me?"

"Dr. Westbrook...that is his door you were knocking on, was it not?"

"You seem to have me at a disadvantage. You know my name, yet I didn't catch yours?"

The man removed his hat, extended his left hand and with a crooked grin introduced himself. "I'm Jeremy Nickels."

Sadie cautiously yet politely shook his offered hand. "Mr. Nickels - what is it that you want?"

"When you see Dr. Westbrook, please have him come see me. Its business...I hope you understand."

A chilling thought came to her. This man was not a good man. She didn't want to show this man any fear. Sadie simply nodded, turned and left by the main staircase.

Partway down the stairs she found Cliff and Jon below holding an intense conversation with the same men she'd seen him with on the street. She consciously decided this wasn't the time or place. Sadie held her head high with masked confidence as she passed through the lobby of the Badger Hotel. She didn't let herself show how upset she was until she got home.

September 18, 1928

Downstairs at the hotel, I saw Cliff with some pretty powerful men. They looked like the same men I'd seen him with yesterday. I do not like this Mr. Nickels. He is a bad man. He made sure I knew he's watching us. I need to tell Cliff of our meeting. I don't think I want to know what he does. My heart tells me he's a good man. I want to believe a man who can be so tender in bed can't be like those he is with.

Sadie finished the passage in her diary when she heard someone at the front door. She knew Lavern was already in bed for the night.

Putting on a robe over her cotton gown, she padded down the stairs to answer the door.

To her surprise it was Cliff.

"I know it's late. May I come in?"

Sadie opened the door for him to enter. Closing the door behind him, she held back all her maddening thoughts and feelings. She didn't want to bombard him with these things all at once.

"Sadie, I know you saw me tonight. Thank you, for not interrupting that meeting. I feel I need to explain."

"Cliff, what have you gotten yourself involved in?"

Cliff hung his head and sighed heavily. He took Sadie's hands in his, and looked into those incredible eyes. "I don't even know where to begin?"

"Who is Jeremy Nickels?"

Cliff's entire body became ridged. "How do you know that name?"

"I wanted to surprise you tonight. He was upstairs watching your room. He not so subtlety introduced himself to me. *He knew my name.*"

Cliff swallowed hard. "He didn't threaten you, did he?"

"No, not in so many words, but he told me he needs to see you."

Cliff pulled Sadie into him and held her tightly. For the next few hours Cliff confessed to Sadie everything; his work in Chicago, his work for Mr. Nickels, and what he and Jon have been doing. He even told her about the men from the War Department he'd been meeting.

"Sadie, I only wanted to keep you safe and away from all of this, but now I think it's important that you know what's going on. You must keep it to yourself. This project will all be over soon, and when it is, I want us to leave here."

"Where would we go?"

"I have family in Poughkeepsie. If you don't want to go to New York, we'll find somewhere else. You tell me. I would gladly give you the moon if that was your heart's desire."

Sadie smiled. "I love you, Clifford Westbrook. It really doesn't matter where we go, as long as I'm with you."

Chapter 18

Cliff had been planning this day for a while, and after hearing Sadie's confessed love for him, he didn't want to wait. There was so much happening at work, but he still found the time to do this special thing with enlisted help from Nebraska.

He noticed the subtle changes in Sadie's appearance and loved her warm glow. She was absolutely stunning.

They drove out to Lake Geneva, where a sailboat was waiting for them at the dock. Nebraska had everything set up, per Cliff's request.

Sadie was so excited. She had never before been sailing. Smiling wide, "Cliff, you don't have to impress me, you already have me."

He flashed Sadie one of his charming smiles, "For you, anything, always."

Sadie loved the peacefulness of the lake.

Sailing out on calm waters, Cliff worked up the courage to propose to Sadie. They sailed around the lake with light winds of 4-8 knots, just enough to fill the sail and jib. The wind gently pushed them along. She noticed the color changes in the water, and told Cliff how spectacular she thought it was.

He found the perfect place to drop anchor, and its sail. Cliff then brought out the Champagne and the basket of treats Lavern had packed.

"Well, aren't you putting on the Ritz!"

He filled a long stem glass flute of bubbly Champagne for Sadie. As the bubbles reached the surface and burst, they tickled her nose.

Cliff got down on one knee. Trembling, he produced an exquisite ring, "Sadie, I fell in love with you the day we met. Fate had brought us back together, and I want you by my side, always." He paused as he took out the ring he had made for her. "Will you marry me?"

Sadie was mesmerized by the breath taking diamond and platinum ring. For a moment she was speechless. "You don't have to do this."

"I didn't say I had to, I said I want to. Say yes; make me the luckiest man alive."

Not in her wildest dreams could she imagine this; Cliff proposing to her. She knew Cliff made her happy, but could he be happy with a former whore who is now carrying his child? "None of this seems real."

Cliff asked in a soothing and caring tone. "What are you so afraid of?"

"I'm afraid this is all just a wonderful dream, and I'm going to wake up."

Holding Sadie's delicate hand in his, and tenderly placing his other hand upon the side of her lovely face; his thumb traced her soft lips, as she gave into his touch and her captivating blue eyes gazed back into his. "I love you, Sadie. I have never felt so alive or happy in my life. I don't want to waste one moment with you. I love you for not only who you are, but for who I am when I'm with you."

Hearing those words come from the man she loved with all of her being was perfect. His proposal was perfect - he was perfect - she was not. Her eyes began to water. *Damn it! I don't want to cry.* She told herself. Sadie looked to Cliff's loving glance. She could feel the true love he had for her and never wanted to let that go. She reached out, placing a hand on the side of his handsome face and gave him her answer. "I will. Forever - I will!"

Cliff grabbed Sadie and held her tight, sealing his proposal with a kiss.

September 22nd 1928

I think I'm dreaming. The most wonderful dashing man asked for my hand. It was so romantic. And the ring is exquisite! Its center stone, a large Old European cut diamond, with a pair of smaller vertically set marquee shape diamonds and 4-round tiny stones set into engraved shoulders. He wants to get married right away. How could I be so lucky to have a man like Cliff, love me? I must be dreaming.

*

"Oh my God!" Katie glanced down at her ring.

Billie stopped reading.

"It's *my* ring! My ring was Sadie's ring? She describes it exactly!"

"That can't be the same ring, Katie. I thought that was Cal's great grandmother's ring?"

The two friends stared at each other in silence.

"Oh my God! Sadie was Cal's great-grandmother?" Billie blurted out. "That can't be right?"

Katie had the feeling she was right about who Sadie was. "Keep reading, maybe we will find out more."

Chapter 19

October 1, 1928

Today was the day. Sadie was so nervous she felt ill.

Father Paul, as a favor to Lavern presided over Sadie and Cliff's nuptials. He saw how much in love they were with each other and was happy to do so.

Nebraska was honored that Cliff and Sadie asked him to attend as their guest. He had worked very hard helping Lavern with her backyard flower garden. The white arbor heavy with pink climbing roses, made a perfect background for the private ceremony.

Cliff caught his breath when he saw Sadie. Her Ivory silken dress draped in layers trimmed in beading hid her condition, but her happy glow showed on her lovely face. He didn't think she could look more beautiful.

The sun was warm and cast a golden sheen in Sadie's strawberry-hair. She held a small bouquet of flowers held tightly with pink ribbon. As she approached her beloved Cliff the butterflies in her stomach calmed. Her shaky hands steadied. It felt so right standing by his side. She knew with all her heart this was meant to be.

Vi stood next to her dearest friend as witness, just as Jon stood up for Cliff. Both were overjoyed for the happy couple.

"I, Cliff, take you, Sadie, to be my beloved wife, to have and to hold you, to honor you, to treasure you, to be at your side in sorrow and in joy, in good times, and in bad, and to love and cherish you always. I promise you this from my heart, for all the days of my life."

Sadie was over the moon. A single tear made its way to the surface and rolled down her peachy cheek as she too repeated her vows to Cliff.

Lavern was so happy, she cried.

Nebraska put an endearing arm around her and handed her a hanky.

October 5th 1928

Although we are wed, we have decided that for my safety I am to stay with Miss Lavern. He warned me things would be stressful until we leave. Tonight, he was to come by for dinner, but he never showed. I am worried that something happened.

October 9th 1928

Everywhere, people were huddled around the radio listening to the World Series; Yankees v.s. Cardinals.

Even Miss Lavern jumped up and down, so excited when Babe Ruth, with a bad ankle, knocked three into the seats during the 4th game. He and Gehrig were great!

While everyone is talking about Babe Ruth hitting 3-homeruns in the World Series, I am privy to something much more important. Cliff says there are things the country isn't ready for. He wants to take me away from this place, but he has to do something first to keep anyone from using what he and Jon created. If it ever got into the wrong hands, he says millions could die. This talk frightens me...the sooner we can leave this place the better.

*

Sadie was busily working in the kitchen, helping Lavern prepare dinner.

"Hello, Beautiful!" Cliff's rich velvety voice made Sadie's heart quicken. Grabbing Sadie in an embrace, he kissed her with such passion.

Her face felt warm, and she knew she was blushing.

Cliff placed a gentle hand on her expanding belly. "How are you doing?"

Sadie covered his caressing hand with hers. "We're doing just fine."

Cliff kissed her on the cheek. "I miss you."

Sadie smiled and then handed Cliff a few plates to set the table.

Cliff gladly took the dishes from her.

"It won't take me long to pack. I really don't have much."

Taking hold of Sadie's hand Cliff said, "Don't worry so much about these things. All I need is you." He smiled, "I hear a touch of excitement in your tone. Are you anxious to leave already?"

"I am, but I'm also sad to be leaving Miss Lavern and Vi. They're family to me."

Cliff kissed Sadie's forehead. "I know love. I promise you, we will come back here many times to visit."

Her heavy heart lightened with his assuring words, and the squeeze of his hand. What was it about this wonderful man that made her believe anything was possible?

November 29th, 1928

Today, as I looked around the Thanksgiving dinner table at the faces of my dear friends, Lavern, Vi, and Nebraska, I know how thankful I really am. I owe Vi and Lavern both so much. I am sad to be leaving them, but they are happy for me. With my family of friends and my new life with Cliff and our baby, I am truly blessed.

Chapter 20

Cliff didn't break for lunch or dinner; instead he waited until the others had all left for some privacy to approach his partner again. "You've got that look. You figured it out didn't you?"

Jon's bloodshot glassy eyes glanced up in acknowledgement. "I did - we did...God help us all, we did! This was the application we needed."

"You're sure?"

"I've run through it three times. If I'm right...and I *know* I am...based on what you and Albert gave me, this will destroy generations not even born yet. It's the most fucked up shit!"

Cliff was speechless. They worked hard to accomplish the most devastating biological weapon and succeeded; however, they couldn't celebrate.

Dr. Schmidt stood in the doorway behind them. Neither Dr. Westbrook nor Dr. Blake heard Schmidt come back in until he spoke. "So - you did it?"

Jon and Cliff turned to see Albert standing behind them.

After a moment of awkward silence, Jon answered. "It's premature to get too excited. It will need to be tested, of course, and that will take some time. But, yes, I think we've got it."

Albert glared at them with a suspicious eye.

Jon simply ignored it and stuck his head back into his notes.

Cliff understood their premise for stopping the enemy before they could hurt an American. He just didn't have to like it.

December 12ᵗʰ 1928

I'm meeting Cliff in the east tunnel. He told me not to wait for him if he isn't on time. I don't know if I could ever leave without him. I know he's scared. He's put on a brave front, but he's in too deep.

There was no way Sadie was going to leave without saying good bye to her dear friend, Vi. After all, Vi saved her life that day, years ago, at the train station.

Sadie's delicate hand rapped on the door.

Vi was surprised to see Sadie standing there, but was glad to see her one last time. "Oh, sweetheart, come on in! Did you come all the way over here just to see me?"

"I had to, Vi. I just couldn't leave without seeing you."

"You know, sweetie, I am a bit jealous of you right now."

Sadie's face lit up. She knew why, and she couldn't be happier. She put her arms around Vi in a large embrace. "Oh, Vi - I love you! I can't thank you enough for being there for me. It's so hard to say good-bye to my best friend."

"Don't you *dare* start to cry! I can't stand tears!"

Sadie held out a cigarette case. "I want you to take this."

Puzzled, Vi creased her brow, and took it.

"There is enough money in there for you to leave town and maybe get a new start."

"I can't take this. You'll need it with the new life you're starting."

"No - Vi, I want you to have this. If I can do it, then maybe I could share a little of my luck with you, too."

Vi's eyes started to water, "Damn it, Sadie! I hate to cry!"

The two embraced each other, as sisters; best friends.

Vi straightened up. Then walked over to her bed, got down on her knees and lifted a loosened board. "This is a great way to hide what you don't want found. If you know what I mean." She gave Sadie a sassy wink.

What Vi said made perfect sense. "Vi, I have something that I'd like you to hold for me. I don't think I should take it with me, and I don't want to destroy it either."

"Ya, sure toots! Do you have it now?"

"No, but I promise to bring it before I meet up with Cliff tonight."

Vi carefully put the floorboards back. "I'll be here!"

Sadie kissed both of Vi's cheeks and left.

Nebraska saw Sadie coming down the stairs, and smiled. "Good afternoon, Miss Sadie!" Then he fetched the door for her.

Sadie gave him a nod, "Thank you, Nebraska!"

*

The night air was cool and crisp. The stars were shining bright jockeying for position with the moon lighting up the sky.

Mr. Nickels stood outside the Blake residence door and knocked.

Charles Blake answered, "Can I help you?"

"I'm looking for your father, Dr. Jonathan Blake."

Charles glanced at the two henchmen behind Mr. Nickels.

With deep persistence, Nickels' added, "If you don't invite me in, it's only going to be worse."

"They can stay here." Charles said reluctantly.

Mr. Nickels gave his men the signal to stay, and followed Charles inside, politely removing his hat.

They sat at the kitchen table, both men leery of the other.

Charles took in every detail of this man, including the silver signet ring he wore. "I told you, my father isn't here."

"I heard you. He has something of mine in his possession I need back."

"Have you checked Deuces? Otherwise, I don't know where he is."

Mr. Nickels was growing tired of Dr. Blake's little games. He clenched his jaw, "I want you to give your father a message for me. He either gives me what he took, or bad things are going to happen."

Charles's eyes narrowed, as he sat forward. His voice angry but low as to not wakeup the house, he slowly enunciating each syllable clearly for the man in black. "Don't - you - *dare* - come into my home and threaten my family. You come anywhere near my family, I - *will* - kill you."

"Just handle your father, and you won't have to worry about it."

The two men glared at each other for a long moment. Charles held his ground, and ended their stare down. "I believe you've said your piece, it's time you leave. I will pass along your message, *if* I see him."

Charles closed the door behind Mr. Nickels, and turned toward the stairs. He felt little Stella had been eavesdropping, but didn't see her there.

The next morning, Charles cornered his father in the garage. "Do you want to tell me what the *hell* you've gotten yourself into?"

Jon considered his son's livid tone, but didn't want to involve Charles. "I don't know what you mean?" Jon said dismissively.

"That Mr. Nickels fella came looking for you last night. Dad - that is *not* a man to fool with."

"You don't need to concern yourself. I've got it handled."

"Handled? That son-of-a-bitch threatened *my* family!"

Jon face showed real anger. "He didn't hurt Molly or Stella, did he?"

"No, but he said or else! What the hell did you do? Does this have anything to do with the outfit?"

"No! He's not the mob."

"Then just give him what he wants."

"I can't give him what he wants. It's too dangerous for anyone to have!

"For the love of God, Dad, tell me what you've gotten us involved in."

"Don't worry; we'll take care of it. It's hidden down below. Trust me; I'll make sure that they won't bother you again."

*

Jon secretly met Cliff in the east tunnel. Both had been taking turns secretly moving and hiding their "formula". With help from Nebraska, they were getting very familiar with the tunnels under Burlington. Even though it was mostly written in code - Stella's code, they weren't taking any chances.

They were able to work their way from one end of town to the other all underground. The gangsters used these tunnels to not only transport their bootleg, but also as an escape. Those in charge of the Government project adopted part of the western tunnels to fit their needs. The tunnel that leads from the bowling alley to Deuces had a gate closing it off; foolishly thinking the locked gate would be respected.

Jon was visibly agitated.

"What's happened Jon?"

"Mr. Nickels has threatened my family if we don't turn it over. We can't let anyone have it."

"Jon, let me take it. I'll be the fall guy. You need to keep your family safe."

"Hey - you have a family now, too! We created it; we'll keep it safe, together."

"I've already taken the necessary precautions. If we don't make it, at least I'll know Sadie and the baby will."

Jon shared a desperate look with Cliff after those words were spoken out loud.

"It's only a matter of time before they figure out our little shell game is a farce."

"We need to destroy those cases of wine, tonight!"

From the dark recesses of the cavernous room, a voice boomed in protest. "No - you won't!"

Quite startled, Cliff and Jon both turned to the sound of the voice.

"I knew keeping an eye on you; Dr. Blake would shed some light on what Mr. Nickels has been up to."

"Well if it isn't Dr. Jeckal's evil twin, Mr. Hide!"

"Dr. Blake, I understand your cynicism, but you need to trust me. I am only trying to help you and Dr. Westbrook."

"You'll have to excuse me, Agent Hughes; I'm having some major trust issues right now!"

"Do you want to tell me about this wine you need to destroy?"

"Not particularly." Jon's eyes narrowed, giving Cliff a sideways glance, unsure of how much of their conversation had been heard.

Cliff asked, "Mr. Hughes, why don't you explain a few things to us?"

With a slight tilt of his head, Hughes shifted his attention to Dr. Westbrook. "Such as?"

Cliff took a bold step forward. "We don't like to be pawns in whatever game you and Nickels are playing. How 'bout some straight speak and clear understanding!"

Hughes' lips thinned as they stretched into a smug grin. "That's exactly what we'd like, Dr. Westbrook; seems to me the only one who knows anything about anything is Mr. Nickels."

Jon retorted, "Then I suggest you find and follow Mr. Nickels."

"This calls for a trust of judgment on both sides. As you know, in the heat of the moment, Doctor, a man is likely to forget where his best interests lie. Have you decided what side you'll be on when this all goes down?"

Jon flashed Agent Hughes a crooked smirk, "Yeah - my side!"

"I strongly suggest you don't do anything rash before I return with my men. We'll be taking the wine and whatever else Nickels had you work on while you were here."

Agent Hughes escorted Cliff and Jon out of the tunnels. Hughes went to fetch his men, while Cliff and Jon headed to the bowling alley.

If they were being watched they weren't taking any chances they'd be seen going near the 480 building. Only they knew there was an access to their lab through the bowling alley.

*

That evening, Nebraska loaded up the suitcases from Cliff's apartment and drove over to Lavern's to retrieve Sadie, and her luggage.

Cliff had given Nebraska his car earlier in the day, and given him strict instructions. *"I'm depending on you. I trust you'll protect my wife."*

Nebraska had a bad feeling, but didn't want to worry Miss Sadie. After all, it was his job, if things did go wrong; he was to take her to Cliff's family in Poughkeepsie. No one would ever know her secret; Nebraska would make sure to keep it. Nebraska respected Cliff and Miss Sadie. He was loyal to them and would always look after Miss Sadie. As far as Cliff's family was concerned, they would think he was their driver.

Sadie was so excited. She was beginning a new chapter in her life with the man she loved and a baby on the way. This adventure they were about to embark on was thrilling, yet scary as well.

She worried about what Cliff and his partner were about to do. Cliff tried to act calm, but she sensed his apprehensiveness. All the waiting was making Sadie nervous.

*

Making their way through the west tunnel, Jon quickly picked the lock on the iron gate. He had done it so often, it was easy.

Cliff kept thinking about his meeting tonight with Sadie in the eastern tunnel; however, this was something he had to do. He couldn't leave until this was finished.

Cautiously they crept down the hallway to the lobby entrance. No one seemed to be around, which left them both with an unsettling feeling.

Cliff absently asked out loud as he stood just inside the lobby door, "What the hell did they do?"

Jon stepped up, peering in over Cliff's shoulder. "Son-of-a-bitch! We need to get to the lab."

The lab's vault door was left wide open. They were shocked by what they saw as they stepped onto the platform. The remnants of their lab, was left in chaos. Even the crude wine vat they had was dismantled.

Jon sprinted down the metal steps and raced to his station. His files had been rifled through, some were missing.

Cliff had followed Jon's lead. Someone had gone through his papers as well.

"I knew it! So help me God!" Jon ranted.

Cliff's attention turned to Jon. "They took everything we had on Zephyr's Kiss."

"Paranoid - my ass!"

"You were right, Jon. That's why we've been running all over town playing these damn games! It's in code; they'll never figure it out. Besides, Nickels believes you've gone mad."

"I need to know if they found it."

"They could be watching?"

Jon spread his arms wide, "Do you see anyone here?"

"Jon, something isn't right. Call it a gut feeling, but this didn't just happen. This was planned and executed."

"They've elected to abandon this lab." Jon flashed Cliff a grave look.

They raced up the steps and down the western tunnel. Everything was dark and bleak. They stood anxiously outside the heavy dungeon-like door. Jon removed his picks from an inside jacket pocket. He feverishly worked the lock. It took some tricky-finger-finagling, but Jon managed to unlock the door.

Cliff followed Jon in. A chill ran through him. "Jon, it's too quiet."

They approached the first cell. Dead. The next cell; the same thing. Five cells, five dead, all with their throats cut. Their blood soaked mattresses leaking onto the floor.

Cliff was thinking it; Jon was the one to verbally confirm it, "That's a lot of blood."

"They aren't letting anyone live to tell what happened here." Cliff watched the color drain from Jon. "Who do you think Nickels and Hughes really work for?"

"I really don't give a damn. Those bastards belong to the same club and I don't mean the Boy Scouts! I think Nickels pissed in Hughes' sandbox and then took his ball away from him. I just don't like us in the middle of whatever this is!" Jon continued to rant, "What they did here, whoever did it, there is no way we can ever let them have that formula!"

They slowly and cautiously worked their way down the tunnel to the end where the crematorium devoured any trace of the victims.

"There is nothing left!" Jon said angrily and kicked a wooden crate across the room. "They took our samples and destroyed the remains. Now what?"

"We need to finish this. We can't let them use it."

Nickels stood blocking the doorway with his .38 aimed at Jon. "I thought I might find you down here."

"What's with the peashooter?" Jon channeled his aggravation in Nickels' direction.

Cliff stood stock still. He wasn't about to be foolish.

"Gentlemen, it seems we have come to the end of your contract. We'll be needing your work, all of it."

Jon spurred, "Looks like you already took our work."

Mr. Nickels' eyes narrowed, "Not all of it. You are holding out on us Dr. Blake."

"I don't know what you mean."

"Tisk, tisk, Dr. Blake. Enough with the games. You have something that doesn't belong to you. You need to hand it over. Now!"

Cliff shared an apprehensive look with Jon. In that moment he knew Jon was about to try something daring. Daring, and stupid.

Jon surprised Nickels with a sudden rush grabbing for the gun. "Run Cliff! Run!"

As Jon and Nickels struggled, Cliff made a break for the open door. He made it through before the gunshot rang, resounding after him. Cliff's entire body flinched and he stopped. Thinking to himself, *"I know I'm going to regret this."* He was scared but felt the need to turn back to make sure Jon was all right.

Cliff found Nickels leaning over Jon's body searching his pockets. Jon's eyes, lost, rolling up as he half heartedly held his bloodied gut. Anger surged through Cliff's veins. He pushed Nickels away from his friend. The sound of steel hitting cement as Nickels' gun slid under a rack. Both men dove for the gun while punching, hitting and pulling on the other. Cliff managed to get a hand on the .38, pulling it out from under the rack. He pushed away from Nickels and stood holding the gun on Nickels. Before he knew it, Nickels got up, lunging at Cliff. He reached across Cliff's arms to wrestle the gun from him. As they desperately struggled with the revolver, Nickels managed to twist it towards Cliff.

A single shot went off.

Both men looked the other in the eye.

Cliff's knees buckled under him. He sat back and rolled to his side.

Nickels took this opportunity to search Cliff's pockets. Neither one had anything of importance. Frustrated, Nickels left the scientists to die in the tunnel.

Cliff managed to crawl over to Jon. Thinking he was already dead, "Damn it, Jon. What in the hell were you thinking?"

Jon's head tipped down in Cliff's direction. His blood-soaked hand slowly moved from his gut to reach out for his friend. His voice was very low, "In my head that went better."

"Crazy, son-of-a-bitch!"

"I'm sorry, my friend."

It was becoming harder for Cliff to breath, much less talk. The taste of copper filled his mouth. He managed to reach out to grab his fedora. Placing his hat upside-down in his lap, he stared at the photo of Sadie he kept in the inside band. Her beautiful smile and those light colored eyes looking back at him. He'd never have another sunset or sunrise with her. He'd never know his child or watch him grow, but he held on to the confidence he had in Nebraska to get Sadie and their unborn child home to his family.

*

Quick knocks sounded at the door.

Vi answered to find a tearful Sadie. "Oh Honey, get in here. What's wrong?"

Sadie shook her head. "He wasn't there! I don't know what to do?"

"Baby girl, that man loves you. He's crazy in love with you. If he wasn't there something prevented him from getting there."

"I know! That's what worries me. I need to go back down there. Nebraska doesn't want me to. I think he knows something and isn't telling me!"

"What were Cliff's words, exactly?"

"He said he'd find a way, and for me not to wait for him. He told me if he wasn't there to just go with Nebraska, and he'd catch up."

"That sounds reasonable. You said you thought he was mixed up with something dangerous. Sweetie, he's probably just trying to keep you and the baby safe."

"I know." Sadie sighed. "But, I have to try."

"I know you do...but you need to trust Cliff. If he isn't there this time, promise me you'll just leave with Nebraska and don't look back."

Sadie's red tired eyes searched Vi's. She nodded in agreement. Sitting at Vi's dressing table, Sadie opened her diary one last time. Sobbing, she penned a few lines.

December 15th, 1928

Cliff wasn't there. I waited until I couldn't any longer. I'm scared. I don't know what happened to him. I'm tempted to go back in and check one of the other tunnels. I'm beginning to doubt myself. Was I in the wrong tunnel? Could he still be waiting for me?

Taking the scarf from her neck, Sadie carefully wrapped the book and handed it over to Vi.

Vi lifted the floorboard, stashing it away forever.

"Thank you, Vi. Where I'm going no one needs to know who I was, just the woman I'm destined to be. I need to leave my past where it needs to be; in the past."

Vi hugged Sadie good-bye one last time. "I wish you a safe journey."

Sadie smiled, "I hope you follow your dreams, you deserve the best."

Vi's heart hurt as she closed the door after her friend. She was truly going to miss, Sadie. The anxious waiting for an inevitable unknown was taxing, on her friend. Cliff always kept his word until tonight. Vi feared Sadie wouldn't have her *happily ever after*.

*

Nebraska knew how much Cliff loved Sadie. Nothing in this world would keep him from meeting her. Something prevented Cliff from keeping his promise. He decided to search the tunnels and find Cliff.

Working his way west through the tunnel system he came upon the iron gate. He had seen Dr. Blake pick it before, but he had no such tools. It was already morning by this time and he would have to return tomorrow night to search the tunnels past this gate. *"Hold on Mr. Cliff. I's coming for you. Just hold on, wherever you are."* Nebraska tipped his head up to speak to God, "Please watch over Mr. Cliff."

*

Nebraska returned the next evening, but this time he came prepared. He jimmied the iron gate's lock and entered. Cautiously making his way to the lab he listened for any little sound and watched for any kind of sign from Cliff.

Once he got to the lab it was obvious it had been abandoned. He continued his search. Nebraska's heebie-jeebies acted up seeing the heavy dungeon-like door standing open. This was not a good sign. He swallowed hard, and tried to gain some extra courage to enter. Nebraska just knew nothing good was passed this doorway. The smell alone was enough to make him want to turn back, but he couldn't. He needed to know what happened to Cliff.

The dimly lit space hummed as its lights flickered. He saw cells lining the wide hallway. Nebraska slowly walked by each cell looking for Cliff. There were dead men, but none of them were Cliff. At the end of this hall was another tunnel. There was a bit more light; however, that didn't make Nebraska feel any easier about investigating.

He found another opened door, and just beyond it lie two men propped up against the wall.

"Mr. Cliff?" Nebraska rushed over to them. "Dr. Blake? Mr. Cliff?" He noticed their blood soaked hands and bloodied bellies. "Oh no, Mr. Cliff! What you gone and do? You got yourself done shot, is what you did!" He knelt down beside Cliff and touched his face. He felt cold and all his color had drained. Nebraska's heart hurt for Sadie and for himself. Cliff was a very kind man and good to him. He considered Cliff a friend. Nebraska sent a little prayer for Cliff's soul.

He crawled over to Dr. Blake and reached a hand to his face.

Dr. Blake mumbled, "Will you pray for me, too?" He coughed hard. Blood came to his lips.

Blake spooked Nebraska. "You's scared me, Dr. Blake. I's thought you's *was* dead! You's got yourself done shot. It's bad, but I's get you outta here."

Fading fast, his words were barely audible. "No, Death is here for me." He looked over to Cliff. "He really loved Sadie. Keep your promise. He's counting on you."

In a somber tone, "I's will, Dr. Blake...and I prays for you, too."

Chapter 21

December 19th, 1928

Cliff had made Sadie promise to leave without him, but she just couldn't do it. She refused to leave with Nebraska. Every day for many days she waited for Cliff in the east tunnel, but he never came. She had to find him.

Cautiously following the tunnel from the bowling alley, Sadie came upon an iron gate. Hesitating, but for a moment, she slipped in barely making a sound. She couldn't believe the beautifully bricked arched ceilings and walls. The eerily quiet hallways that jutted out in a couple different directions made her anxious.

She tried to remember what Cliff told her about the lab and the secret tunnel that was heavily secured. She tried the first door on her right. It was a large vault door, and opened easily, a little too easily.

Peeking in she was in awe of what she saw. This was Cliff's lab. It was amazing and impressive. She stood still, listening to the still air. Nothing.

She moved on to the next door. On her left was a doorway. She peered inside. It looked like a reception area, yet had racks of wine. The bottles looked very familiar. *Nebraska's wine?* She thought to herself.

Sadie swallowed hard. She was frightened, more than she wanted to admit. Cautiously venturing down the tunnel to where it veered off to the left, Sadie had a strange feeling. A troubling feeling. She came upon a wooden door with heavy metal hardware. It was ajar. The tiny hairs on the back of her neck stood on end. Her hands began to tremble as she reached for the knob.

The odor beyond this door was disturbing. The silence was deafening. It was difficult to see much of anything. Everything was in dark shadow, but what she did see behind the cell doors was horrifying. Now, she was beyond scared, but Sadie was desperate to find Cliff. She eagerly searched each cell, revealing the faces of several lifeless men.

Halfway down the corridor a large warm hand covered her mouth as the arm grabbed her from behind pulling Sadie tightly into his body. Sadie's blue eyes, wide with fear searched the dimly lit space.

"Shhh!" The voice she heard was Nebraska's.

Nebraska kept his hand over her mouth, keeping the screams he knew would come, silenced. He moved with her into an open cell. He was glad he followed her. He couldn't let her see Cliff's body.

The silhouette of a corpse on the cot was prominent. Sadie's body shifted nervously in Nebraska's arms.

Again he whispered in her ear, "It's not *him*, Miss Sadie.

She nodded her head, okay.

They stood quietly for a long period of time just listening to the dark, patiently waiting. Nebraska was unsure if anyone would return, but he wasn't going to stick around to find out.

Slowly, Nebraska removed his hand from Sadie's mouth. He placed a finger to his lips, letting her know to be quiet. She took Nebraska's hand and silently followed him out.

She desperately wanted to finish her search for Cliff, but knew she needed to go with Nebraska. They made their way out of these tunnels. Sadie had made Cliff a promise she knew she must keep.

*

Sadie frantically pounded on Vi's door.

There was no answer.

Letting herself in, Sadie quickly closed the door behind her. She was so scared she leaned against the wooden door trying to catch her breath. Tears stained her face. *This can't be happening! Why?*

Sadie ran to look out the window. Nebraska would be coming for her soon.

Sadie turned focusing her gaze upon the floorboards that hid her diary. Quickly she dug it out and sat down at Viola's dressing table to jot down her last words in her diary. After all she was about to start a new life. There was no need to bring her past along with her, but maybe she needed to leave some words for Cliff, or Vi or someone in the future who needs to know what happened here.

December 19th, 1928

I never should have looked for Cliff. Our lives are now in danger. If they haven't found me yet, they soon will. I am so scared. What will happen to us? They have secrets hidden in the tunnels. What I saw in that room, I never should have seen. I had to know if Cliff was one of them. They can't allow me to live after what I discovered. It's not just me anymore.

Sadie heard Nebraska's horn and returned the diary to its resting place in the floor and put the floorboards back, before leaving.

Sadie hustled down the stairs, and then quickly stopped in her tracks. Three men, one with a large silver signet ring on his right hand were waiting in the lobby of the 480 building. The man with the ring wasn't Mr. Nickels, but she felt they were cut from the same cloth.

"Shit! How am I getting past them?"

Vi had seen Sadie and ran after her. She found Sadie frozen in place on the stairs. "Are you okay, Sweetie?"

Sadie shook her head, no.

Vi peeked around the corner to see the men in black. The one with the ring left, leaving the other two. "I've got an idea. Just go with it, and when you see an opening, you run like hell girl."

Sadie hugged her friend. She loved Vi like a sister and would miss her terribly.

Vi and another gal played it up, giggling and stumbling down the stairs. They carried on, overly flirtatious with the men in black. Pawing and kissing, and teasing them. When they weren't getting quite the response they had hoped for they started a cat fight. Making such a scene in the lobby everyone took notice.

Sadie took this opportunity, to slip right past the men. She knew better than to run.

Nebraska was parked in the alley, engine running, and lights off.

Looking over her shoulder as she rounded the corner Sadie bumped right into someone. Turning to apologize, her eyes quickly grew wide with fear when she saw it was Mr. Nickels.

"Just the woman I've been looking for. I believe you have something of mine."

"I don't have anything of yours."

"Well, here's the thing. Dr. Blake didn't have it. Dr. Westbrook didn't have it. That leaves you."

"Where's Cliff?"

"I'll let you see him, as soon as you hand over the formula."

"Formula? What formula?"

"Please do us both a favor, don't bother lying to me. Just give it to me!"

Tears filled Sadie's eyes and ran down her cheeks. This man truly frightened her. "I don't have what you're asking for. I don't even know what you're talking about."

With quick anger, Mr. Nickels struck out and backhanded Sadie across the face.

Sadie yelped. She quickly grabbed her cheek, which he left a stinging mark with his ring. She turned back holding her face, the last thing Sadie saw was Mr. Nickels collapsing to the pavement.

Nebraska stood over the man holding a tire iron firmly in his grasp. A faint moan came from Mr. Nickels, and Nebraska hit him again for good measure. This time he didn't make another sound.

In a daze Sadie held her cheek. Her tear-filled eyes looked to Nebraska.

Nebraska looked down at the tire-iron he held. He dropped it where he stood.

"It's time to go, Miss Sadie." He said putting an arm around her.

Nebraska held the door open for Sadie.

"Cliff isn't coming is he?"

Nebraska sadly shook his head no. "I'm afraid not, Miss Sadie."

Those chilling words changed something inside Sadie. She complied with Nebraska, sad, numb and confused, Sadie climbed into the car. She wanted to deny it, but knew it to be true. The pain of this sudden loss pushed through. Tears blurred her sight and stained her cheeks.

He slowly backed the large sedan down the alley, as its lights illuminated the lump on the ground before them until it faded into the shadows. Nebraska shifted into gear and pulled out onto Pine Street heading south towards Chicago. "Everything is going to be okay, Miss Sadie. Mr. Cliff told me just what to do if something went wrong. I'm taking you to his family in Poughkeepsie."

Sadie gently rubbed her belly, stoically staring out the window.

Nebraska observed something dark filling Sadie from down deep. "Please don't, Miss Sadie. Mr. Cliff wouldn't want this for you or the child."

Sadie still didn't respond. Her stillness was upsetting to Nebraska. He didn't want her to retreat inside herself.

They drove for over an hour in silence. Somewhere over the Illinois border Sadie blurted out, "Pull over!"

Her outburst startled Nebraska, and he quickly pulled off the side of the road.

Sadie couldn't get out of the car fast enough. She bolted out of the car before Nebraska barely had his door open. She was off like lightning. Sadie ran, and ran, and ran, as Nebraska called after her. Sadie stumbled and fell. He caught up to her kneeling and screaming in a frozen field. She wasn't physically hurt, but the ache she felt inside was horrendous. Sadie kneeled, clutching herself and wailed. She was a complete wreck. All her dreams had been dashed before they even started.

Nebraska sympathetically approached her and got down on one knee in front of Sadie.

She looked up to him with blue eyes filled with pain.

Nebraska held her shoulders, and said with a strong conviction, "Leather is a product of the dead; we don't want a heart of it. Everything else of it...is useful!"

His words seemed to calm Sadie. The odd look on her face softened as she grabbed hold of Nebraska, hugging him and crying into him. He hugged her back, letting her cry herself out. When she was done, he picked-up Sadie's exhausted tiny frame in his arms and carried her back to the car.

Part II

Chapter 22

Present day - Burlington, WI

Curled up on the couch, with their glasses of wine, Billie closed the red-leather diary and set it down. They had read the diary, page by page, twice.

Katie was in awe. "Christ, Billie, can you imagine the life this girl had? I have to get back down there! You're coming with me, right?"

Billie stared blankly at her friend.

Katie took a sip of wine. "What is *that* look for? Come on - *please*! I really need you. You've been by my side this entire time...don't make me finish this alone!" Katie changed direction with a sudden burst of random thoughts. "Hey - you know what's puzzling to me? We found her diary in the 480 building, but she lived and worked at the Plush Horse. How the hell did her diary end up in the floorboards of the 480 building?"

Billie's face contorted into a scowl.

Katie jumped up, grabbed the plans she drew of the 480 building off the dining room table and brought them into the living room to show Billie. "Look at my drawings! I created these based off the photos you took, and our measurements." She then jabbed a finger to an irregularity on the print, "See here, there has to be a space behind this wall on the second and third floors. I want to know what that space is. Aren't you curious?"

"Well, yeah...but..."

"But? Oh come on - aren't you at least a little bit curious? There is something this building is hiding, and I'm going to find out what it is!"

Billie rolled her eyes. She knew she would eventually cave-in, and follow her friend back down into the tunnels anyway, but first she had to attempt to be the voice of reason. She let out a heavy sigh, "I can see going back into the building, but I don't know about the tunnels?"

"Fair enough! Let's start here," Katie pointed to the third floor plans, "and work our way down."

"When do you want to start?"

"How about first thing tomorrow morning?"

"Don't you want to wait until the guys get back?"

"Billie, Cal left for D.C., and Jack is up north fishing with TJ and Midas."

"Exactly! Katie, what if something happens? We've been lucky so far, but I've got a bad feeling this time. I can't put my finger on it, but it's there."

"Okay, I'll let Paul know I'm working back inside the building and we'll tell Mary what we're doing. At least someone will know where we are. Would that make you feel better?"

"I can't believe we're doing this!"

*

While Billie was trying to trace the path of the pneumatic tube system; Katie was on the third floor standing in front of the bar, just staring, motionless for a long time. There was something more than its lavish canopy adorned with beautiful Tiffany glass framed in fretwork and the fancy scrolled and carved designs that drew Katie's attention.

Billie returned to the third floor proudly waving a bag of glow sticks. "Ah-hem!" Billie cleared her throat to get Katie's attention. "You haven't moved since I left. What are you looking at?"

"I'm not sure." Katie answered. Her gaze still fixed on the mirror at the back of the bar.

"I brought these!" Proudly, Billie held out the glow sticks and a mirror with a telescoping handle. "I thought we might get a better look at what's inside."

Katie raised a brow, "You've been dying to do that since you found that thing!"

The impish gleam in Billie's eyes and her crooked grin told Katie, that it was. "Okay - go ahead. Let's see if anything is in there."

Ripping open the package, Billie snapped a stick and shook it before letting it drop down the chute. She held the mirror over the opening and tried to make out where it had stopped. "It doesn't look like it made it all the way down. How far do you think that is?"

Katie tried to gage. "I don't know, maybe the first floor?"

"Okay - but that means it's in the wall somewhere. I didn't see any drop box - did you?"

"No - I'm sure over the years things have been covered up, like the hidden door to the basement."

"Can we open up the wall down there?"

"What?"

"I want to open the wall."

"Billie!"

"Well - something is plugging it. Aren't you curious, even just a little bit?"

Katie chewed the inside of her cheek debating with herself.

"Aw come on! I know it's against your historical preservation code or what-not - but you said it yourself...through the years things have been covered over and changed." Billie could see she was wearing Katie down. "You even said the answers are in this building!"

"It's not fair when you use my own words against me, BJ!"

Satisfied, Billie smugly grinned from ear to ear.

"Don't get too excited, if we're going to be opening up walls I'll need to run this by Paul first." As Katie dialed Paul, Billie put on her biggest pouty face. Katie tried not to giggle at Billie's shenanigans. Paul answered.

"Paul, its Katie. I'm inside the 480 building trying to trace where the pneumatic system goes. I think it's hung up on the first floor. What kind of lenience's do we have for opening up the walls?"

Paul was silent for a moment on the other end of the line. "If you feel it is important to finding more on this building then do it. Just do it in a respectful manner."

"Thank you, Paul, I will."

"Let me know what you find."

Katie hung up in time to see Billie doing a little victory dance. "Nice, Billie."

Katie dug in her canvas bag of miscellaneous gear and pulled out a length of chain. She tied a long piece of string to it.

"What are you going to do with that?"

"Here," Katie handed it to her. "I want you to drop this down the tube until the chain hits the blockage. Then bounce it a little bit so I can hear it through the wall. I'll know where to drill."

"Okay, I can do that."

Katie followed the sound down to the first floor. She drilled a couple of large pilot holes in the general area she thought the shaft would be. The third hole leaked a soft glow.

Using a hammer, Katie knocked enough plaster away to the wire mesh and lath beneath. Snipping the mesh out of the way it was easy to break away the old dry lath boards revealing the tube she drilled a hole through. Together they made the hole a little larger to expose more of the tube. Now using a Sawzall, Katie cut the section off at the top of the pilot hole and then about three-feet down.

Billie took the three-foot section and tipped the glow stick out. The pneumatic shuttle was wedged in tight. Billie looked inside at what could be lodged in there, from the other end. "Katie, take a look at this."

Shining a light inside the tube revealed papers protruding from the side of the shuttle. Katie cut off another section of the tube closer to the shuttle. They tried to push the blockage out through one side. "That didn't work. We should take it back to the house with us and put it in a vice, then push it through."

Billie shrugged her shoulders and tossed the section of blocked pipe into a canvas bag. Katie broke and shook a glow stick before dropping it down the last section of tubing. There wasn't much to see. It was difficult to make out but there was definitely a bend to the left. "We'll have to see where that goes later."

Looking at the mess she made, the floor was dusty and littered with old plaster and pieces of wood. Katie picked up the larger pieces while Billie used a hand broom and swept up the rest.

Billie gave a large dramatic sigh, "So much for that. What's next?"

"Back up to the bar, I guess."

"What's with you and that bar? Don't get me wrong it is beautiful and all, but it's just a bar."

Katie was shaking her head. "No, I think there's a way to get behind the wall from the bar. The exterior measurements don't coincide with our interior measurements. I think the bar's mirror is a two-way and there's got to be a space behind it."

"Are you serious?"

It was Katie who was smiling now. "Come on - let's see if I'm right!" Katie grabbed Billie's hand and dragged her back up the stairs.

Once again they stood at the bar, staring. Katie took a hand and ran it across all the panels. Billie opened every door and drawer.

"I don't know what you expected to find here, but it's not here." Billie walked passed, heading for the other room.

Katie begrudgingly agreed. "I suppose - but there has to be a way to get behind this wall!" She watched Billie walk away. "Where are you going?"

"If you must know, I have to pee!"

Katie cocked her head and raised a brow. She waited for Billie to figure it out. *Three, two, one...*

"Hey! Oh - yeah!" Billie giggled, and then she stopped.

Katie expected Billie to turnaround and walk right back out, but when she didn't, Katie called out to her. "Billie - what are you doing?"

Silence.

"Billie!" Katie was puzzled. She got up to see what Billie was doing. As she entered the men's room, she found Billie running a hand over the dingy white subway tiles on the far wall. "What are you doing?"

Billie backed up to where Katie was standing and pointed to a section of tiled wall. "Take a look at that wall. Look real closely."

"What am I supposed to be looking for?"

"You'll know it when you see it. Just look where I was standing."

Katie stared at the rectangular patterned dingy white wall so long her eyes were going buggy. Then she zoned in on the faint outline in the pattern. A smile grew upon her face. She stepped up to touch the irregularity in the grout lines. "I feel it! There's a hot wisp of air coming through."

They tried to trace the outline of a removable panel. Nothing else seemed to stand out.

"I know what we need - smoke!"

"Smoke?" Katie asked but quickly understood what Billie suggested, "Yeah - smoke!"

"It's time for lunch anyway, and I *really* have to *pee*! Let's run over to the Sci-Fi for lunch and maybe Mary will have something we can use."

*

After lunch they returned with a fat smudge stick of White Sage that Mary Sutherland had given them. Billie lit the sage and waved its smoke over the wall. Some of the smoke seeped in the tiny crevices of broken grout lines.

Katie traced the lines where the smoke had sucked in or blew in little swirls and waves. They managed to mark out an area of tiled wall that could be a hidden door. Now, if only they could figure out how to open it.

Looking around the narrow, tiled room, a row of white porcelain urinals lined one wall. The urinals sat side-by-side on the floor and drained into a trench drain in the floor. The floor in front of the urinals was made up of a wide strip of tiny hex tiles bordered by large black tiles. The entire bathroom was white except for the black accents. The plumbing ran out the top of each and tied into the next with every set of three sharing a flush handle; save for the one on the end. On this last urinal, the plumbing was a little different; it had its own flush handle. Katie knew the water had been long ago shut off, but she flushed the handle anyway.

Turning to the sound of a click beside her, the wall in which she had marked popped, just a fraction.

Billie giggled with glee. "How cool is that?"

Katie gave one side a push and the approximately 3' X 5' center hinged section of wall opened, revealing the narrow space just beyond. "I knew there was a way to get behind here!"

Retrieving their flashlights, Billie followed Katie. They stepped over the threshold, and into the hidden space. The space was no more than a 36" wide hallway that ended at a tight metal spiral staircase. They approached the spiral stairs. Katie was right; the bar's mirror was a two-way.

Katie peered through the dirty glass and imagined what it was like to spy on a room filled with gambling men, and gangsters.

Billie held out her arm in front of Katie, "Check it out - I've got goose bumps! I wonder how long it's been since anyone was back here?"

Slowly taking the winding stairs down to the second floor, they stepped off. They walked only a few paces before they saw a small framed box in the wall. Several wall studs over was another framed box. Katie tried to open it. After wriggling with the latch she managed to pull it open. It was a peep-hole. They counted four in all.

"There are four rooms on this side and four peep-holes. They probably had prostitutes here!"

"And the perverts watched?"

There was no need to respond. It wasn't really a question, more of an observation, and knowing what Sadie wrote in her diary - it was a likely conclusion.

Taking the spiral stairs down to the first floor there was no landing, the stairs continued down to the basement level. Here they found themselves behind an entrance blocked by cinderblocks.

"Wasn't this the Badger Hotel?" Billie asked.

"Yes, and now it's Coach's Bar and Grill. We haven't been in this part of the tunnels."

Billie reached out for Katie's arm, "I don't think we should go too far."

Katie turned to Billie, seeing her eyes held deep concern. "Okay, we won't go too far. I just want to see what's around that corner."

"That's all? Then we go back."

Katie nodded her head 'yes'.

The length of tunnel to the corner was only about 200 feet, and Billie was anxious all 200 feet of it. Katie shined her light around the corner. There wasn't much to see. Some conduit hung down, a broken light fixture lay on the path, and lots of cobwebs reflected the light she directed that way.

"Yep, looks real promising! Let's go back!"

Katie laughed. "What's with you?"

"I just don't like it. We can explore that tunnel another day, just not today. Okay?"

"Okay."

*

Paul Richter had been in Lake Geneva when Katie called to ask about opening up a wall. He'd never known Katie to be so insistent on demolition inside a historical structure. Out of curiosity he came through Burlington and stopped in to see what Katie had found. The 480 building was unlocked, but Katie wasn't around. On the first floor Paul saw the vertical hole she made in the wall. She had done a nice job of keeping it between the studs and all the debris had been swept up. He called out for her, but there was no reply.

By the time Paul had made it up to the third floor, Billie and Katie were just passing by the back of the bar's two-way mirror. They stood behind the mirror and watched Paul. He had pulled out his cell phone to make a call. "I don't know what she found. She's not here. She may have gone back down in the tunnel." He paused to listen to whoever was on the other end of the line. "I'll let you know as soon as I know." He hung up and slipped his phone back in his pocket. He hesitated. Staring into the bars mirror, the girls held their breaths. It was as if he could see them through it. After a moment, he turned and walked out the door.

In a hushed whisper, "Oh my God, what do you think that was that all about?"

Katie was asking herself the same question.

The air was hot and stifling in that narrow space, but they waited a few minutes to make sure Paul had left before they exited the sanctuary of the hidden room. "Let's take that section of tube I cut out of the wall and go back to the Victorian. I want to see what's in there."

Katie had been relatively quiet and incessantly chewed the inside of her cheek. Billie couldn't take much more of the silence. They only had a few blocks to walk, but it was making her fidgety. "What's Paul's story?"

"Huh?"

"Your boss, Paul...what's his story?"

Katie made a face at Billie's interruption. "I don't know. I worked with him on a historical project back in college, and then Constance got me back in touch with him to work on this project."

"How does Cal's mother know him?"

"Not really sure...I guess they're old friends. What's with the twenty-questions?"

"That's two questions! What's with your brooding mood all of a sudden?"

Katie unlocked her door, and was immediately greeted by a very happy Hondo. The large German shepherd wagged his tail and nosed Billie. Katie made sure to lock the front door. "I better let him out before we get started on this."

Katie returned through the back door with Hondo at her side. Billie and Hondo followed Katie into the basement. The basement wasn't just an ordinary basement. It had been transformed into a functional office and work room with lots of lighting.

"Wow! Cal really out did himself! I guess having all that time on his hands paid off."

Katie smiled, she was proud of Cal's hard work; however it was a long and difficult time for Cal. Being suspended ate Cal up inside. Building this space was more of an outlet for his stress than anything else. "Yeah, Cal does nice work. He's very good with his hands."

Billie giggled, "I bet he is!"

Katie just shook her head. "Nice." She patted the canvas bag, "Let's crack this puppy open!" The gleam in her eyes sparked.

Billie pulled the tube out of the bag and placed it in a vice mounted to the workbench. Katie secured it at about a 45° angle. "Hand me a 2"X2" out of that barrel over there." Katie pointed to the corner under the stairs.

Billie retrieved a short piece of wood and handed it to Katie.

Placing the wood into the tube she tapped its end with a hammer. Slowly the shuttle, which was lodged in the tube began to move. "Man - that thing is in there tight!" Katie tapped it even harder. Finally she got it out. The shuttle was stuffed full and some of the papers had held it open.

"What is all that?"

Taking her time, Katie pulled out a pocket book wrapped in note papers. After all these years the papers were dusty and curled up. After all the pages had been laid out, Katie placed a heavy book on top to flatten them out. The pocket book was bound in brown leather embossed with gold-leaf letters, 'J.B'.

Goose bumps raised and tingled down Billie's arms again. "I wonder how old *that* is."

"Looks pretty old." Katie opened the little book. There were scribblings that looked like math equations or scientific notations. Some of it was legible; at least the first half of the book, but then it became very cryptic.

"What the hell kind of language is *that*? It looks alien!"

"I don't know what any of this is." Katie pulled a few sheets of paper out from under the book. They wanted to spring back into their curled state, but she managed to hold them open to see its writing somewhat legible. "This says Fluorine: 9th element. Toxic. Fluoride poisoning and related ailments: dental fluorosis, skeletal fluorosis, sterility, birth defects, cancer and brain damage."

"Fluoride? You mean the stuff they put in toothpaste and our drinking water?"

"Well, that's what this says. I can't imagine why any of this would be in an old building."

"Holy shit! Okay - so what does a whorehouse/gambling house/florist/Western Union and barbershop have to do with that?"

"I wonder if Stella from city hall might know. There isn't much she *doesn't* know about Burlington."

Chapter 23

It was 6 a.m. Wednesday morning, and the sun had already peeked over the horizon turning the remainder of the cool night's air heavy with moisture. Katie was very excited to meet Stella for breakfast at the Sci-Fi Café. The tote bag with the famous *Water Lilies*, picture by Monet she was carrying, contained the little book and note pages she and BJ found. She strolled down the uneven gray sidewalks, swinging it to and fro; carefree and happy all the way downtown.

Stella was standing outside the café's door smoking a cigarette when Katie arrived. "G'd morning, Stella!"

Stella's husky voice, deep from years of smoking answered back, "Good morning." She turned to exhale the smoke away from Katie. Looking down at the tote she carried, Stella asked, "Is that it there?"

Katie's eyes held a spark of intrigue. "Yes - and I can't wait to show it to you!"

Taking one last drag on her cigarette, Stella then snuffed it out in the ashtray left on the decorative ledge of the building.

Billie was already inside having tea with Mary. Brad, Mary's husband, and cook greeted them from behind the counter when they stepped in. "Morning ladies!"

"G'd morning, Brad!"

"You ladies having some breakfast this morning?"

"Of course! I already know what I want, too!"

"Let me guess - your usual?"

"You got it!"

"Billie ordered the same thing. You girls are so predictable."

"If your breakfast sandwiches weren't so good - we wouldn't be ordering them!" Katie gave Brad a little wink as she led Stella to the table where Billie and Mary sat to make introductions. "Stella, this is Mary Sutherland, the owner of this establishment."

Mary happily greeted Stella. "Hello, Stella!" She turned to Katie with a large smile, "We've run into each other many times over the years."

"Yes - yes we have!" Stella returned the smile and laughed.

"Sit. I'll get you a cup of coffee!" Mary hustled over to pour a cup for Stella, and hollered over her shoulder, "Katie, you want one too, or did you want tea today?

"Coffee would be great - thanks!"

"Now don't start without me - I don't want to miss a thing!"

Brad came over to take Stella's order. "I better get your order in now, wouldn't want to interrupt this Powwow!"

"Let's keep it simple - I'll just have what everyone else is having."

"Are ya sure? I've got biscuits and gravy!"

"Goodness no...I'm not *that* hungry!"

"Not even a half order?"

Mary sat back down and gave Brad a look.

"Okay - the boss is back - better get to it!"

Billie placed Sadie's old red-leather diary in front of Stella.

Katie took out the little brown book with the gold initials, J.B., along with the flattened yellowed pages.

Mary grabbed the pocket book and flipped through it. She was just as excited as the girls.

Stella sipped her coffee as she scanned through the diary. She paused on a page. Her face changed as she tried to recall something from the past, then her face softened. "Miss Lavern." She pursed her lips, and tapped the top of the table to help her remember a little quicker. "Oh - I remember her! She was my teacher! She ran a boarding house for women back in the day. Lavern was something else! I remember that old boarding house; it had the most beautiful gardens. Everyone gossiped about her being a widow and having a black man work there with all those single women, was something terrible." Stella chuckled, "I'll never forget Nebraska - he was the nicest man you'd ever want to meet! I loved that man. He'd tell me stories, and he taught me how to play cards so I could beat Gramps." Stella laughed at the fond memory. "Though I think Gramps let me win, I still had great fun playing his games. I seem to recall playing cards with Gramps and Nebraska, once or twice. I think we were in the basement of one of these buildings. Anyhow, I'd sneak Nebraska penny candy and that was our little secret. Yes indeed, he was pretty special to me. Lavern couldn't pay him much but he'd work for her and she taught him to read. I'd ride my bike over there and she'd always have something sweet for me. When she'd make fudge, she'd let me lick out the bowl. Those were the days."

Billie sat quietly listening to Stella's tale, but was baffled. *How could Miss Lavern have been her teacher?*

"We found this diary in the floorboards of the 480 building. It was written by a woman named Sadie, who we know was a prostitute here in this building, but then she moved in with Lavern when she fell in love with a man named Cliff." Katie stated.

Stella chewed on that for a minute. "You know, my mind isn't what it used to be, but I recall there being two cat-houses in town. Deuces, which was also a gambling house my Gramps liked to go, and the Plush Horse, which was in this building. I was a wild child then. I could leave the house and be gone all day running amuck. But Gramps told me to stay clear of Deuces. He didn't want me hanging around there. I always wondered if he was with the mob, since everyone knew they owned it and he was there almost every day."

Mary set down the little brown-leather book. Stella glanced at it and picked it up. She ran her fingers across the gold embossed letters, J.B. They all noticed the change in Stella's face as she opened the book. Stella was quiet; for a long time she remained quiet, turning each page of that book.

In almost a whisper, Stella finally spoke. "Where did you ever find this?"

Billie piped up, "In the craziest place - a tube in the wall of that old 480 building!"

"It was stuffed in a shuttle and sent through the pneumatic tube system and got lodged," Katie sort of corrected Billie.

"This was my grandfather's!" She closed the little book and touched the embossed letters again. "J.B., my grandfather's name was Jonathan Blake." She opened the pages of the book. "See here." She said pointing to the alien script, "He and I used to send each other secret messages using this code. It's been decades but I think I can figure out the key to it."

Katie and Billie were beyond surprised, and Mary was just as caught up in Stella's tale as they were.

Brad brought over their breakfasts and topped off Katie and Stella's coffees.

Stella ran her fingers over the words on every page as if to absorb their content through sheer touch. These were her grandfather's words, written with his hand. She felt a long lost connection to her past.

Billie's entire body was tingling. She was glad she was drinking tea; she would certainly be bouncing off the walls if she'd had caffeine. "Stella, whatever happened to your grandfather, or Nebraska?"

Stella's eyes watered. "I don't know. I was about 9-years old the last time I ever saw either one of them. Matter-of-fact, they disappeared the same time."

"Wait - you were 9? That would make you..." Billie started doing the math in her head. "You mean to tell us your 94-years old? We all thought you were in your 70's!"

Stella laughed. "Don't go telling anybody. I like my job and they may force me into retirement. Then what would I do? Shrivel up and die!" Stella reached a hand across to Billie's. "Back then women never discussed their age, and I still don't."

Billie blurted out the first thought that came to her mind. "And you're still smoking?"

Stella's quick wit shot back, "Well I can't live forever!" She smiled, half chuckling.

Katie redirected the conversation back to the original topic. "Stella, do you know if that building was used for anything else?"

Stella turned to Katie, "Only what we have a record of and of course the 'not to be mentioned' Deuces. I was warned by both my father and grandfather, to stay away from that building. 'Don't go snoopin' where you ain't got no business being in the first place.' They would tell me." With a caring hand she closed the book and patted its cover. "May I take this with me? I'd like to see if I can remember the cipher we used."

"Yes, of course." Katie smiled.

After breakfast Katie was feeling pretty confident Stella would come through. The two sleuths walked 2-blocks from the Sci-Fi to the 480 building.

Katie inserted the key to unlock the door, and hesitated. She looked back over her shoulder, down the street to the west and then to the east. She didn't see anything suspicious but she felt it. It was an uneasy feeling, just like the one she had before Eddie took her.

"What's wrong? Are you all right?"

"Yeah, it's nothing." Katie pushed open the door and quickly locked it back up behind them.

Billie gave Katie a suspicious eye. "If it's nothing, then why couldn't you lock the door fast enough? I saw you looking around...you think someone is watching us?"

"Ever since we watched Paul make that phone call I've been a little guarded."

"Have you talked to him?"

"I did. I told him there wasn't much to report back, just yet."

"I thought you trusted Paul?"

"I do...I think? I don't know. Paul has been great - a little too great! There's something about this building he hasn't told me and I don't like secrets!"

"Just ask him about it."

"I will - but after I hear back from Stella."

"Okay, Dora - what kind of adventure are we going on today?"

Katie just flashed Billie an impish grin as she walked over to the hidden door to the basement. "Shall we?"

"I knew it! I just knew you were going to go back down there. You know if anything happens down there while the guys are gone, we are never going to hear the end of it."

"What could possibly happen?"

"Aww - don't say that! You're going to jinx us!"

"So think positive!"

"I am. I'm positive we're going to get into trouble."

Katie started to laugh at Billie's sarcasm when her cell vibrated. She looked to see who the caller was. "Hello."

"Katie? It's Constance, Dear. I know Cal is out of town, but I was hoping you'd be free for dinner tonight."

Katie looked to Billie. "No, no plans. I'd be happy to have dinner with you."

"Very good. Say 6:30, my house?"

"I'll see you at 6:30."

Constance hung up, and Katie put her phone away. "That was odd."

"Why was that odd? I thought it was very nice of Cal's mom to ask you over for dinner."

"Are you trying to tell me *it's me?*"

Billie gave Katie a smartass grin and opened the basement door. "Well, what are you waiting for? You've got dinner tonight with your mother-in-law to be."

Katie shook her head and followed Billie down. They turned on their flashlights. No matter how many times they came down here, there is still that eerie factor that doesn't go away. Katie shined her light on the wine racks. "Are there bottles of wine missing or is it just me again?"

"No - I've been taking a bottle every time we come down here."

"Is it any good?"

"I don't know - I just thought they were cool old bottles. I haven't opened any of them."

"Come on, I want to check out that first tunnel; the one that was blocked. I'm hoping after the explosion it may have opened up."

Their lights fell upon the crudely blocked tunnel; and just like Katie had been hoping, a large crack in the block was present.

"I'm going back for my tools!" She turned to go back up.

"Katie - don't you dare leave me down here!"

"BJ - they're just upstairs."

"That's alright, I'll come with you."

Returning to the blocked entranced, Katie set down her bag of tools. Katie started tapping and chiseling away at the crack. A few pieces crumbled exciting Katie to push and pull on some of the loosened block, making a few more fall. They set their lights down and worked to remove enough of the blocks for them to get through. The sound of block hitting concrete echoed through the inner chamber.

After they made a large enough opening, they shared a look. Dust hovered in their beams of light.

"Ready?" Katie asked.

"Can I go on record that this is now freaking me out? I just got the chills!" Billie said looking through the opening they just made a moment ago.

"Stay close - you'll be fine." Katie took a step over the rubble into the dark tunnel. She panned her light along the narrow tunnel walls as she waited for Billie to come through.

Katie found a fuse box a short distance in. "I wonder?" Pulling the lever, a snap and hum began to radiate down the tunnel. A few flickers of light, and then the soft glow of lights in tin housing buzzed to life.

Surprised, the two sleuths shared a look.

"Come on, let's see where this goes."

They followed through a narrow passageway and down a few concrete steps to a sublevel. The air was cool and musty. The first opening was on their right. It looked like a large bank vault door. It was open and covered over with cobwebs.

Katie used her flashlight to rip a large hole in the flimsy, insect incrusted, dusty curtain of webs.

"Eeew! There better not be a giant spider to go with this!"

"Billie!"

"Well...I don't like spiders!"

They stepped onto the metal grated landing and looked out to the lab below them.

"Wow! What is this place?"

"I don't know, BJ, but I bet Stella's Grandpa's book has something to do with it."

Billie followed Katie down the stairs and back into time.

"Katie, do you think this was Cliff's and Jon's lab?"

"It certainly looks like it could be." Katie walked up to a workstation and touched the dingy glass beakers. "Look at this stuff!"

Billie was distracted by a wall of buttons and dials. She reached out to turn one of its knobs. "This looks like an old radio or something. It's huge! I wonder what this was for."

"Well, it does look like a transmitter/receiver of some sort, but look at the copper coils." Katie pointed out.

Billie giggled, "That looks like part of a still over there. Maybe they were high-tech bootleggers!"

They walked around the lab, snapping a few pictures. There were some drawers pulled out of two of the desks, and their contents discarded all over the floor.

Billie picked up an aged slip of paper. "Hey, here is more of that alien script!"

"This must be where Stella's Grandfather worked." Katie scanned the lab. "I wonder where the access to the pneumatic tube system is."

Billie added the slip of paper to her bag. "I thought you said the tube turned out to the east. I'm not very good with direction down here, but I'd have to say we're too far west."

"No you're right."

Snapping the last shot, "Okay there went a roll of 36!" Billie removed the roll and replaced it with a new one. "Onward and upward?"

"Yeah, I want to look around here some more, but let's see where the tunnel takes us."

They climbed back up the stairs, exiting through the torn webs and followed the tunnel to the right. Immediately to their left was another room. This door was also open. It was a small room, consisting of tall gray metal filing cabinets, two desks with chairs and a console with a coffee pot and three coffee cups. The filing cabinet drawers were all empty. Nothing in any of them. The desks had a few odds and ends, but no files. There was a calendar with some notes filled in on certain dates.

"I wonder if any of these dates match the ones in Sadie's diary."

Billie snapped a couple of pictures and then held out her hand. Katie handed her the calendar and she slipped it in the duffle bag, too. "Well that was anticlimactic."

"Okay, moving on!" Moving back into the tunnel, they continued westward.

Trailing behind, Billie felt a presence. She walked a little faster to catch up to Katie. "Did you tell Paul we were coming down here?"

"Not exactly, why?"

"No reason."

Katie stopped suddenly and Billie, who was looking over her shoulder, ran into her. "Billie!"

"Oh sorry."

"Really, Billie? No one is following us. We're the only ones down here."

Billie gave Katie an '*I don't necessarily believe that*' look.

Katie shined her light back down the way they just came. "See, nobody's there."

"I know what you're saying, but I'm telling you I've got this feeling. I don't know what it is, but I'm not liking it one bit!"

They continued on, treading lightly for Billie's sake. It wasn't long before the hair on her arms stood on end and a chill ran down her spine as they stopped in front of a dungeon-like door with heavy metal hinges. "Well - that's not ominous at all!"

Katie tried the handle. Nothing.

"It's locked." Billie stated the obvious.

"I see that!" Determined to see what was behind the door, Katie took out a pry bar and a hammer.

Billie was just as curious as Katie, as to what was behind the mysterious door; however, she had a really bad feeling about this. Reaching out for Katie's hand, she stopped her. "Wait! What are you going to do?"

Looking down to the pry bar in her hand, Katie answered mockingly, "I'm going to open it with this."

"Maybe we shouldn't. Something bad is in there, I feel it."

"Billie, it's been closed up for decades! Whatever you think is in there, it's been gone for a long time."

"That's not what I mean! I just have this feeling."

Katie measured Billie's concerns. "I want answers for all of this, and something tells me we'll find them behind this door!"

Billie dropped her hand. "Okay, but I don't think we're going to like what we find."

Using the hammer, Katie tapped up on the bar into the first hinge. With a bit more force she managed to pop the hinge pin. She then worked at the bottom pin and pulled that one. The middle pin was more of a challenge and with a loud snap, the pin came up. An uneasy look passed between them before the old heavy door made a loud creak in protest as it fell open. They shinned their lights into the eerily quiet tomb-like space, lined on both sides with small prison-like cells. The air was stuffy, and there was an unfamiliar odor but neither one spoke of it.

Stepping with caution, they checked in each cell. The first two had heavily stained bare mattresses on metal bed frames. Shining a light in the third cell, Katie caught her breath as Billie gasped.

"Are those real?" Billie whispered.

Katie respectfully approached the skeletal remains sparsely clothed in almost disintegrated fabric. She trained her light on it to get a better glimpse. "It's real."

"Oh my God - Katie!"

"I know, Billie."

"Do you think it could be Cliff?"

"It's possible."

Their light revealed another skeleton in the forth cell. They found the same image in the next five cells. When they got to the end they realized there was another exit leading into a wider hall.

"I don't like this." Billie protested in a hushed tone.

"I don't either, but I need to follow it."

"Kate - there are seven skeletons behind us - behind bars! What the hell was this place?" Billie looked to Katie for answers, but she was just as clueless as Billie.

"Can you get a shot inside each cell? Then we'll see where this goes."

Billie reluctantly nodded. She felt cold and out of place here, in this surreal world they discovered. As she framed each shot she noticed many things. The dark staining on the mattresses, the ones holding skeletal remains were rotted out. Two of the skeletons were secured to their beds, and three of them had some odd deterioration of their bones. She snapped the last shot in the last cell, "Who would do this?" Billie turned to find a strange faraway look on Katie's face, "Are you okay?"

Katie nodded her head. "Ready?"

"Are you sure we should continue alone? Maybe we should call someone, like the authorities?"

"We will call someone - after we make it all the way to the end of this thing!"

Billie still felt a presence, but decided not to tell Katie. She figured Katie would just chastise her for being paranoid, so she kept it to herself.

Beyond the swinging clinic doors was a wide hall. There was what looked like old gurneys and a medical cart with old fashioned glass syringes.

"What in the world is this?" Billie picked up a funky metal syringe with a trigger, a bulbous colored glass top feed vial with copper ends, and a very long needle. "This looks like something from *Doctor Who*!"

"Billie, put that down! *Doctor Who* didn't exist back then."

"Well it looks like something I'd see on an episode of *Doctor Who.* It looks like it's out of time and place."

"Oh my God - are we really having this conversation about *Doctor Who*, now?"

"I'm just sayin'!"

Katie let out a heavy sigh. "Can we?" She made a hand gesture to move on.

"Fine!" Billie sulked. "Just sayin'!" She mumbled under her breath.

"Really?"

"I'm anxious and when I'm anxious I need to talk! I just can't help it!"

"There is another set of swinging doors up ahead."

"Katie, this is really creeping me out. It was bad enough exploring the tunnels on the east side, but this is crazy scary shit. We read Sadie's diary, we find hidden passages in the building, and dead bodies in cells. What the hell?"

"Are you done?"

"Probably not."

Katie smiled. Billie rambled on a lot, but she was glad her friend was down there with her. She too, felt whatever it was Billie felt and wasn't saying. She reached out to push open one side of the double doors. There was a creek and a slight hitch in the swing which made Katie hold her breath for a split second.

Billie stopped directly behind Katie. Neither one said a word. At the far end of the room was a crematorium. Wooden crates stacked up on one side. A laundry cart bulging with abandoned clothing. A glass jar containing what looked like human teeth with gold fillings, sat on a desk. These things weren't what stopped the girls from entering. The two skeletons slumped on the floor wearing tattered suits before them; however, froze Katie and Billie in their place.

Many things went through their minds. Neither needed to say it, but they both knew it in their bones, these were the remains of Clifford Westbrook and Jonathan Blake.

Katie made the first move to enter this room, Billie couldn't move. She was frozen with an over whelming gamut of emotions.

Shedding more light on the skeletons, Katie noticed a hat. There was a photo inside the hat of a woman. "Billie, come look at this."

Teary-eyed, Billie slowly sauntered in.

"Take a shot of them and of the hat, just like it is. If I'm right - Cliff is the one with the hat, and if that's Cliff, that's a photo of Sadie."

Billie mechanically snapped photos of the room; the Crematorium, the crates, the cart of clothes, the desk with the jar of teeth, and the two skeletons.

Katie took a closer look, but couldn't really tell what happened to them. Their clothes were quite deteriorated. "They could have been shot? It's kind of strange to have them lying so close together." Looking around the room of doom, "What were they doing to get themselves killed?" She spotted a long forceps and brought it over to the remains. Getting on her knees, she carefully lifted the delicate tattered jacket away from the bones. There was a leather wallet in the inside pocket. Cautiously she pulled the wallet from the pocket. It was hard dried up old leather, but she was able to unfold it. She found a faded piece of paper. "It's a New York driver's license, issued to Clifford Westbrook. It is him!"

"I wonder how the seven guys in the cells were killed."

"The cops will have to figure that out. After all this - I still don't understand what any of this is. It looks like a laboratory of some sort and a prison hospital."

"I wish Sadie's diary said more about what it was Cliff was working on." Katie picked up the hat with the photo in its hat band. "Maybe Cal's mother knows something. I'll have to ask her about some family history tonight." She plucked the photo from the hat and turned it over. "It says, 'With all my love, Sadie'." Katie flipped the picture back over.

Looking at the photo of Sadie, Billie commented. "She was very pretty."

"Yes - she was."

Chapter 24

Katie nervously rang the bell on Constance's door. Constance, as charming as ever answered letting her enter. "I'm so glad you could make it on short notice."

"Thank you for the invite."

Constance was always dressed immaculately. Her Navy and white sweater-set with Navy blue dress pants were finished off with a string of pearls. Of course Katie was pretty sure the pearls were real and her outfit was couture.

Feeling a bit under dressed, wearing jeans and a blouse, Katie followed Constance into the kitchen. "Something smells delicious!"

"Thank you, I love to cook and it's rare I get to cook for someone other than myself."

"I see where Cal gets his cooking skills."

Constance wore a large warm smile. "Cal is a very good cook. I actually think he has surpassed me in culinary skills."

Katie didn't know what to say to that. She just returned the warm smile. "Can I help you with anything?"

"Yes - you can help me eat. I hope you're hungry." Constance handed Katie a plate. "I hope you don't mind, we'll be informal tonight and eat out on the sun porch. It's such a lovely evening."

Katie's mouth watered. She didn't realize how hungry she was by skipping lunch today.

Constance opened up the oven to reveal the herb encrusted lamb chops.

Katie took a rack of 3. They smelled delicious, yet their lightly pink tender appearance in contrast to protruding rib bones was a bit much after what she saw today. She added a large spoonful of garlic mashed potatoes with bits of red peal, and steamed asparagus to her plate.

Constance poured Katie a large glass of French Bordeaux.

Waiting for her hostess to make her own plate, they moved out onto the sun porch. Constance was right, it was a lovely evening.

"How are things going at the 480 building?"

Katie swallowed and took a sip of wine before answering. "Well, interesting."

"Oh?"

"I think that building holds lots of secrets."

"How do you mean?"

"Besides the hidden basement that led to the tunnels the bikers used? We found a hidden space behind the bar on the third floor which led to another hidden space on the second floor and down to the sublevel on the back side of Coach's."

"That does sound interesting. When you first found the basement, didn't you say there were racks of old bottles of wine down there? Did that give you any more information on the history of the building?"

"I know there were mobsters who owned it back in the '20s, and it was called Deuces. They had the gambling on the third floor and prostitution on the second floor. Apparently the businesses on the first floor were legit; a Western Union, florist and barber shop."

"Wow - what a history! I suppose the wine in the cellar was their bootleg."

"More than likely." Katie tried thinking of a way to bring up Sadie and Cliff. She looked down at her engagement ring and played with it. After a few moments of silence she had to ask. "This is such an incredible ring! What can you tell me about Cal's great-grandma?"

Constance saw Katie fidgeting with her ring. "Grandma Sadie? Constance chuckled, "My goodness where do I begin?"

Katie's heart began to pound hard in her chest. *It was Sadie!*

"My grandmother was a character. She was a strong independent woman, much like yourself. That's why I felt it so fitting that Cal asked for the ring to give you."

"Do you have a picture of her?"

"Of course, Dear. Let me grab the family album." Constance left the room.

Katie took a large gulp of wine for courage. If this was the same Sadie - how was she going to tell Constance that her grandmother was a prostitute?

Constance returned with a heavy photo album and the bottle of Bordeaux. She sat down beside Katie to show her the old family photos. The first page showed a beautiful woman with a pretty smile and sad eyes. She held a little bundle in her arms.

"Who is the baby?"

"That is my father."

"So, Sadie was your father's mother?"

"Yes, and..." Constance flipped to a photo out of place. "Clifford was his father."

"Are there any photos of the family together?"

"Sadly no. That's actually a tragic story."

"Oh?"

"You see, Grandma Sadie married Cliff here in Burlington. He had sent a letter back home letting his family know he was sending his pregnant bride home with their driver, Nebraska and he would be catching up after he tied up some business he had here in town. Nebraska delivered Sadie to the Westbrooks, and stayed on as Sadie's personal assistant, but Cliff never made it. Through the years, the family sent detectives here looking for Cliff but apparently he and his partner, Jon both just disappeared."

"What kind of business was Cliff in?"

"I was told he was a scientist working with the War Department. He and Jonathan Blake both were. Grandma Sadie even came back to Burlington many times looking for Cliff. She swore the government took him away from her. Mind you, back then they thought Sadie was touched in the head, but I always believed her stories. They were a little crazy, but too crazy *not* to believe. My father was raised by Sadie and Nebraska. Sadie never remarried. She only had one love in her life and that would forever be Cliff. Nebraska was a black man, yet Sadie treated him like family. My father learned many things from Nebraska, including how to make wine. Even though the Westbrook money came from shipping and paper mills, that's where our money comes from, the wineries."

"Cal never told me that."

"He doesn't like to talk about it. The money and stature never impressed him or his father. They are a lot alike in that way." She turned a few pages back to point out Nebraska. He was older, but a handsome man.

Katie tried imagining Stella as a child, playing cards with Nebraska and Jon. The thought made her smile. She took this opportunity to show Constance the photo she found in the old fedora. "I want to show you something." Katie took the old photo from her purse, and handed it to Constance.

The astonished look on Constance's face surprised Katie. "I've never seen this picture of Grandma Sadie before. Where did you get this?"

"In a hat."

"In a hat - what hat?"

"The one I found in the 480 building."

Constance looked up from the photo of Sadie to Katie. The expression on her face changed. "Kate, I have a confession to make."

This was certainly a strange turn of events. Katie was puzzled; she thought she was the one that needed to confess.

"Grandma Sadie set up a shell corporation and purchased that building back in the early 1930's. Our family has held onto it all these years knowing the answer to whatever happened to Cliff and his partner were inside that building. I did have a hand in having Paul Richter hire you, because I knew you wouldn't quit digging. He highly recommended you and I agreed. When you found those tunnels, I had high hopes. But then you stopped talking about the details of your research."

In a soft sad tone, Katie said, "I know what happened to Grandpa Cliff."

After all these years, Constance felt overwhelmed. She took a large sip of wine and looked to Katie for the answer.

"First I need to show you something else. I don't know how to tell you, so I'll just let you read it." Katie pulled the old red-leather diary from her purse and gave it to Constance. "This was Sadie's. Billie found it in the floor boards on the second floor of the 480 building."

Constance carefully took the book in her hands and opened to the first page. She quietly read her grandmother's words. Her eyes grew with surprise and then shock. Her eyes met Katie's. "Does Calvin know?"

"No. I wasn't sure myself until today."

Closing the diary, Constance held it tightly in her hands and took a deep breath; partly because of relief to finally getting some answers, but also because more dark secrets were about to be revealed. "Tell me about Cliff."

"Billie and I found the skeletal remains of two men wearing suits today. One had a fedora in his lap. That photo of Sadie was inside the hat band, and I found a New York drivers license issued to Clifford Westbrook inside the wallet from the same skeleton."

"Where did you find the remains?"

"In the first tunnel leading west from the basement. When we went down there the first time it was crudely blocked up, but then after the mayor blew up City Hall we found a large crack in it. I chiseled away at it until I made a hole large enough to crawl through. We found a lab, an office and something I don't know how to describe."

"Katie, I'd like you to take me down there."

"Constance, it's...it's really disturbing. I haven't told Paul about it yet, or reported it to the police. I haven't even told Cal!"

"Let's not be hasty." Constance reached over to grasp Katie's hand. "Cal is preoccupied working on an old case in D.C. It's not necessary to interrupt him about this. I'd like to read Grandma Sadie's diary first, and if this is his grandfather, maybe I should be the one to tell him."

Katie nodded her head in agreement. After all, it was their family business.

"Good. Now then, I think we should call Paul to meet us at the 480 building tomorrow morning. I do hope you'll understand if I don't want the police involved, just yet."

"May I ask why the secrecy?"

Constance reached for the bottle of Bordeaux and refilled their wine glasses. Settling in she composed herself.

Katie patiently waited for Constance to tell her what all this was about.

"I'm going to tell you what has been told to me through the years. I do have some firsthand knowledge on the matter coming right from Grandma Sadie." She placed her hand on the old red-leather diary. "Maybe after I read this I will have a better understanding of things." Constance met Katie's eyes, "I assume you have already read this?"

Feeling like she had pried into the most personal of family secrets, Katie answered softly. "I have."

"Let me skip to the nuts and bolts of why the 480 building is so important. Grandma Sadie married Dr. Clifford Westbrook, a scientist working for the War Department. Grandma Sadie claimed there was an entire facility under that building where he and his partner, Jonathan Blake both worked. They were brought on from Chicago to head up project Zephyr."

"Zephyr? The wine that is down in the cellar is called Zephyr's Kiss!"

Constance paused. "I didn't hear anything about them making wine. I was told they were researching the affects of Fluorine and its uses for the War Department."

"We found some old notes with information on Fluorine, and it's pretty horrific."

"I believe what my grandfather was working on got him killed. Grandma Sadie always said that what Cliff and Jon created they felt was too dangerous for anyone to have. Cliff loved Sadie very much, and wanted to protect her and their unborn child, so he was going to take her away from here and go back home to Poughkeepsie. On the night they were to meet in the eastern tunnel, Cliff never showed. Sadie was so stubborn; she refused to leave without him. About a week later, against Nebraska's warning, she ventured down in the tunnels looking for her beloved. She found a small prison where all who were in their cells had their throats cut. She never found Cliff, but conceded to leave that night with Nebraska. I was told, Cliff's boss was a bad man, and almost prevented Sadie from leaving. If it weren't for Nebraska who knows what would have happened."

"So that's what happened to the other seven."

"Seven?"

"There's a tunnel lined with cells on both sides. We found seven skeletons behind the barred doors. You can see it for yourself tomorrow."

"Is that where you found Cliff?"

"No - not in the cells, but further down. He's in a room that was used for cremation." Katie could tell this was far more than what Constance had thought it would be.

"Before we get lost in our stories, let me call Paul."

"Why Paul?" Something wasn't adding up. It could have been Constance he made that call to, except Katie was having some real reservations about all of this.

"Paul has been working with me on this, on and off for a few years now. He's a trusted friend." Constance got up leaving Katie alone on the sun porch.

She couldn't help the sudden distrust she had with Paul. In the past she and Paul were friendly and she looked up to him as her mentor. Her perception of him had suddenly changed since she witnessed his strange call. Looking back down at her ring and fidgeting, Katie realized with all that Sadie had been through, it *was* the perfect ring for her. As beautiful as it was, there was a deeply flawed yet impressive story behind it; the tragic love story of Sadie and Cliff. She would make sure her love story with Cal has a very happy ending.

*

"Paul, its Constance. I hope I'm not disturbing you?"

"No, not at all. What can I do for you?"

"Katie found Cliff!"

"She did? When?"

"Today. It is a crime scene, but I have convinced her not to involve the authorities just yet."

"What do you need me to do?"

"I want you to meet Katie and me at the 480 building tomorrow morning. She will take us to the lab."

"Does she know anything?"

"I have filled her in on some things."

"What time tomorrow?"

"Make it 9:00am. No need to be there too early."

"Is there anything you need me to bring?"

"I'm not sure what we'll need until we get down there."

"Ok, have a good night, Constance."

"You too, Paul." Constance hung up the phone. Taking the peach pie out of the refrigerator, she made up two plates. She returned to the sun porch to find Katie staring out the window. "Dessert? I made it myself!"

"Wow - you've really out done yourself!"

"It's Grandma Sadie's recipe." She gave Katie a warm smile.

*

Paul glanced out the window of his lake home. Checking the time on his watch he figured the math in his head for London time, and placed a call to J.C. Smith. It rang a few times before he answered. "Mr. Smith, the lab has been found."

"Very good," was all the disembodied voice on the other end said, before hanging up the phone.

Chapter 25

Katie had tossed and turned most of the night. Flashes of intermittent dreams of Sadie and Cliff mixed into the present left Katie dizzy. She glanced at the red digital number on the bedside table; 3:20 a.m. *"Ugh!"* She plopped her head back down into her pillow. Rolling over she reached across to Cal's side of the bed. It felt lonely not having him beside her. Katie wished Cal was there so she could talk things through with him. After all *he* was the detective. What she and Billie did, felt more like a Scooby Doo adventure. The more she thought about all the silly, crazy things she and Billie had gotten themselves into, she had to giggle. Then the image of Cal's face and that stern look he'll give her once he finds out, made her laugh even harder. It felt good to laugh. It cleansed the soul. Snuggling with Cal's pillow, Katie was able to fall back asleep.

The buzzing cell phone vibrating across the tabletop woke Katie. With one eye open the caller ID showed it was Billie. She answered not fully awake, "Mornin', Billie!"

"Did I wake you?"

Why is it when people call late at night or really early in the morning they always ask if they woke you up? Usually everyone denies it although their voices betray them. Stubbornly Katie answered, "Yeah, you did. What's up?"

"Sorry...breakfast?"

Katie forced her other eye open and looked at the clock. It was already 7a.m. "Let me get dressed. Sci-Fi?"

Billie giggled, "Is there anywhere else?"

"Not for us." Katie hung up the phone. She wasn't sure if that was rude or not, but decided not to waste her time thinking about it. *Damn I'm tired!*

*

Billie was in the back with a cup of hot tea talking with Brad. They were the only two in the café. Katie helped herself to a large cup of coffee. No need for messing around with a small one today.

Taking one look at Katie, Billie commented. "Wow - you look grumpy!"

Brad turned to look at Katie. He nodded a 'good morning'. "Just let me know when you're ready."

"I didn't sleep well."

"How did dinner with Constance go?"

Katie gave Billie a look as she blew across the top of her coffee. "Interesting."

"Well?"

Katie finally took a sip of hot coffee and winced. She scooped some ice out of her water glass to add to her coffee and stirred. "We were right, Sadie is Cal's great-grandmother, and this was her ring."

"Oh my goodness! That's...wow! What else did she say?"

"I gave her Sadie's diary. It was only right; after all it was her grandmother's. She filled me in on some family history and showed me a family photo album. She told me that under a dummy shell corporation, Sadie purchased the 480 building back in the '30s looking for answers to what happened to Cliff. Over the past few years Constance and Paul have been looking for the underground facility to find the answers Sadie never could."

Billie's big blue eye grew wide, "What? Really?"

"I'm supposed to meet them at the building at 9 this morning and take them down." Finally being able to take a large sip of coffee, Katie smiled; it tasted really good this morning.

"I thought you had doubts about Paul?"

"I'm kinda torn when it comes to Paul, but Constance says he's a trusted friend. I have been through so much this past year I'm not sure I can trust my instincts anymore."

"You're instincts seem pretty good to me."

She gave Billie a genuine smile, "Thanks, Billie!" And then waved Brad over. "I think we're ready for breakfast."

"Let me guess...your usual?"

The girls giggled, "You know us so well!"

"Like I said - predictable!"

*

Although Paul had a key to the 480 building, he and Constance were waiting on the sidewalk out front when Katie arrived. She felt better after she told Billie about meeting them this morning, at least someone would know where she was. The new uneasy feeling she had about Paul was still there; nevertheless, she'd try to hide it. Katie was almost embarrassed by it. She noticed Constance wasn't in her usual attire. She wore blue jeans, a t-shirt and tennis shoes with a denim jacket slung over her arm, and her hair pulled back. She greeted them with a friendly smile and opened the door.

Constance had been inside a few times but today was different.

"Where do you want to begin, on the third floor where the hidden passage is or the basement?"

Paul was a little taken back by the mention of a hidden passage on the third floor. He was surprised Katie had kept that detail from him. He remained silent, and let Constance decide the course of this venture.

"Please take us down through the basement and then the sublevel." Constance seemed excited yet calm.

Katie gave a subtle nod, before pushing on some detail on the paneled wall which then opened allowing them access. Turning on her flashlight, she turned to Constance, "Watch your step. It's a narrow passage and the steps are short."

Constance nodded her head. "Lead the way." She took her first step back into time with promise to finally get some answers. The metal railing wasn't much, so she put her hands out feeling the cool stone walls all the way down.

Paul followed closely behind Constance.

Panning her light to the bottom of the steps for Constance, Katie made eye contact with Paul. It was accidental, but Paul sensed something. She quickly looked away and focused on Constance.

Once they made it to the bottom, Katie turned her light to the wine racks. Paul followed suit. Constance went right to the rack and pulled a dusty bottle from its rest. She wiped away the grime, revealing the label; Zephyr's Kiss. "Katie, it's just like you said." She returned the old bottle to its place.

"The entrance to the tunnels is behind that rack over there. It's a tight fit, Paul; maybe you could help me move this rack out a little more for Constance."

"Of course."

With Paul's muscle they pushed the heavy rack out another foot and a half. Katie slipped through first, then Constance and Paul right behind her.

Shining her light to the right, Katie said, "If we go that way it'll take us to the underground bowling alley and to the other tunnels leading out to the river, but since the explosion I haven't even tried to go back through there." Then she shinned her light to the left. "We are going this way."

They came to the crudely blocked entrance and climbed though the hole Katie and Billie made the day before. Following Katie a short distance they paused at a fuse box on the wall. She flipped the lever. A snap and hum began to radiate down the tunnel. A few flickers of light, and then the soft glow of lights in tin housing buzzed to life.

Constance and Paul both were surprised.

Paul turned to Katie, "How is it even possible for there to still be power on down here?"

"I don't know. Billie first found power on in the bowling alley. She just saw a switch and flipped it on. When I saw this box, I figured what the hell."

Paul gave her one of his 'I'm impressed' looks, just like he did when she first interned for him. Katie tried not to let that cloud the suspicious feelings she was having about him.

They paused outside a large vault door. Katie held open the hole she had made in the heavy cobwebs hanging in their way, letting Constance through. Paul stayed right behind her. The three stepped onto the metal grated landing and looked over the railing down to the lab below.

"This is the lab? Not in my wildest dreams would I have guessed Cliff worked down here like this. This is incredible! It must have been absolutely futuristic for them back in the '20s!"

Katie led them down the metal stairs. Constance and Paul wandered around looking at everything. Paul was busy picking up some scattered pages dusty on the floor, while Constance went to each of the stations trying to decide which one was Cliff's. Katie got her chance to look around a little bit more. She stood over the heavy wooden remains of something. Billie was close, she didn't think it was a still; it looked more like a wine vat. Looking around the lab, she saw Paul playing with the wall of knobs and buttons. Constance was sitting on the floor reading a few of the pages Paul had picked up. This was the second time Katie had been down here and it did feel surreal to her. *"What was it that Billie said? Out of place and time."* It was very fitting.

Constance stood up, dusting off her jeans. She rolled the papers in her hand, "Shall we continue with the tour?"

Katie felt that was an odd comment. Maybe Constance only meant to keep things light considering. She led them back up the stairs and through the curtain of cobwebs, a little way down to the door on their left. "This was their office."

Constance quickly started to open the drawers to the filing cabinets, as Paul checked desk drawers.

Katie commented, "There's nothing here. We looked in all the drawers yesterday. Whatever was here was removed a long time ago."

Katie caught the very disappointed look on Paul's face. Although Constance had heard what Katie said, she continued looking through every drawer until she saw for herself that there was nothing there. Katie stepped out into the hallway and waited for them to do their own search. A few minutes later, Constance and Paul immerged silently. Katie took that queue to move along. It was this next part of their excursion Katie was dreading. The closer to the dungeon-like door she got, the drier her mouth became. It was here, standing in front of its opening that the hair raised on Katie's arms. It felt like static electricity running across her skin. She paused, and turned to Constance. "Before we enter this section of the tunnel, I have to warn you it's quite disturbing."

"I understand, Katie."

Katie saw how Paul reached out for Constance's hand in support. After all these years, Constance was finally going to know what happened to the grandfather, she never got to meet, only hear stories about. She motioned for Katie to lead the way.

The heavy door was hanging by its lock off to the side. Katie panned her light, as they shuffled through the entrance and stopped just shy of the first set of cells. Constance took in the dark shadowed recesses along both sides of the tunnel. The first two cells were empty except for the heavily stained mattresses on metal bed frames. The next cell; however, gave Constance pause.

"I see it, but I can't believe it. They just left them down here all these years. How very despicable!"

"There are six more just like him."

"These are the men Grandma Sadie told me about. The ones who all had their throats cut." Her voice was low and melancholy.

Once they got to the end Katie held open one of the swinging doors. The lights were somewhat brighter in this area. The hum from their tin housing was hypnotic. The old gurney, the medical cart and all its tools were just as they had been left 85-years ago. Slowly Constance took it all in. She ran her hand down the length of the old gurney. As she inspected the medical instruments on the cart, her fingers brushed across each one.

Paul and Constance were both eerily quiet, too quiet for Katie who was used to Billie's constant banter. Katie waited by the entrance to the crematorium. She felt the electricity brushing up against her; it was vibrating, and silent. Her knees began to shake. She began to wonder if it was just nerves or if Billie was right about feeling a presence down here. Katie didn't believe in all that hokum like Billie did. She had to see it to believe it. Whatever it was, she felt it; and if she had to make a guess as to what it was, she'd say it was plain old nerves.

Constance must have noticed Katie struggling with something. She approached Katie, placing a gentle hand on her shoulder and asked, "Is everything alright dear?"

Katie was overwhelmed with her discovery from yesterday, and here she was back there today showing Constance the remains of her grandfather. Katie's voice was small, and waivered just a bit, "Cliff is right behind this door."

Constance embraced Katie, and whispered motherly in her ear, "Thank you, for this Katie. You have no idea how much this means to me."

Katie didn't know what to say. She stood frozen; not scared, but definitely unsure of herself at that moment.

Paul stepped up and placed a caring hand on Katie's shoulder, "You've done a great job, really." They shared a look, and she could see Paul's sincerity. Then he opened the last swinging door for Constance.

For a long time Constance just stared at the scene before her; two skeletons wearing tattered suits. Their leather dress shoes weren't in too terrible of shape in comparison. Other than the position of their bodies, they could have just been laid to rest, dressed in their Sunday best. While Constance studied the two skeletal remains, Paul investigated the rest of the room.

Katie couldn't see everything Paul was doing from where she stood; however, she did hear Constance speaking to the grandfather she never had the chance to meet.

Chapter 26

It had been a long day and now that everyone, except the custodian had gone home, J.C. Smith poured 50-year old Chivas Regal three fingers deep in a Waterford rocks glass. He loosened his Zegna tie and sat back in his Bespoke leather desk chair. He turned his handmade leather chair to face London's night skyline. It wasn't his best scotch, but after the day he just had, it would do. He raised a brow when his cell phone rang interrupting his peace; it was Paul Richter, in America.

"Did you find what you were looking for?"

"No. Dr. Westbrook's remains, and we believe the other to be Dr. Jonathan Blake were down in the facility; however, everything was gone. They took the files and all trace of any samples I'm sure they had, and left the bodies. There are seven, not counting Westbrook and Blake."

"Does the girl have it?"

"I don't think so. She came clean about finding the underground facility, and a hidden space behind some of the walls. I will check that out tomorrow."

"You know what you have to do."

"Yes, Sir."

The line went dead. Paul put his phone down and stared out his lakefront windows. He liked it here. He liked the people, and through the years had grown fond of Constance, but he had a job to do.

*

Constance was very grateful Katie brought her down into the underground facility. She understood why her grandmother was so obsessed with the 480 building. Now that she had Grandma Sadie's diary she could learn more about the amazing woman she knew.

The hot shower felt good. Constance made a pot of tea and settled into bed. She had read the first entry the day Katie gave her the diary, but she wasn't ready to read the rest of it. After today, she was. Opening Sadie's journal back to the first entry, she read it again. It saddened her that Sadie had such a traumatic history. The entry on how she met Viola made her smile. Entry after entry played with Constance's emotions. She drank her tea, in between fits of laughter and tears. She couldn't put it down no matter how tired she was.

Constance felt reconnected to her grandmother. She had hoped Grandma Sadie was looking down upon her and smiling, now that the truth was revealed. That thought gave Constance a warm, happy feeling.

She knew they would have to report what they found to the authorities. Only then would they be able to put their loved ones to rest. She thought about Stella, and how she would feel knowing that her grandfather did not just abandon her family, but was killed protecting them. Constance had so much she needed to tell Cal. She made Katie promise to let her be the one to tell him. She knew this was not the time; she'd have to wait until his return.

Although they found Cliff and Jon, they never found the cursed formula which got them killed. Sadie always insisted it was too evil for anyone to have. She claimed Mr. Nickels; the man who headed up Project

Zephyr was a traitor. Seeing what they did today, Constance believed the formula and all other evidence to it was long gone. They wanted to hide what they did, sealing it forever in a tomb. She smiled thinking about Katie, and her determination to get to the bottom of things. Sadie and Katie are not blood related but they both have similar qualities, including being strong-headed. *"Oh Calvin - Katie really is the perfect girl for you!"*

*

After Cal had called to say good night, the big Victorian was too still. Hondo had climbed on the bed to keep Katie company, except she still couldn't sleep. He was stretched out on Cal's side of the bed, quite comfortable and sound asleep. Katie gently stroked his soft fur and watched him sleep.

Too much had happen this week. She wanted to fill Cal in on everything, but Constance was right; it was necessary for him to focus on the job in D.C. He needed his closure, too. Katie sighed, and glanced at the time. She wondered if Billie was awake. Caving in she picked up her cell to send Billie a text. *R u up?*

A few moments later a text came back. *Doctor Who marathon - giggles.*

Katie rolled her eyes and smiled. She just needed to talk, so she called.

Billie promptly answered, "Hey - how did it go?"

"Just like it did when we found it!" Katie paused, "Constance was...different."

"That's understandable."

"Yeah."

"How did it go with Paul tagging along?"

"Awkward at first, but he was really there for Constance."

"Okay...there's something you're not telling me. What happened? I hear it in your voice."

Katie was momentarily silent.

"Are you chewing on your lip?"

Katie had to laugh, "Nooo..."

"Come on, you know you can tell me anything."

"It's just that Paul seemed to be looking for something."

"What would he be looking for? I mean, it's really cool to explore those old tunnels, and knowing that it was a government facility from back in the 20's! After all, he is an architect."

"I know he's an architect, and yes, knowing what we do about it, it is pretty cool...but he was searching for a file or papers or something."

"Maybe he was helping Constance find Cliff's formula?" There was silence on the other end. "Katie - you still there?"

"How would he know about that?"

"I don't know - Constance could have told him."

"I don't think she did."

"Do you think the formula is in the book we gave Stella?"

"We need to find out if Stella figured out that alien script."

"Why would Paul be looking for that? It's Jonathan Blake's book, so as far as I'm concerned it's in the right hands." Billie's tone was steadfast.

"I'm happy Constance can have closure now that she found her grandfather. But...I feel there's something else going on with Paul."

"I think with all the secrecy surrounding the 480 building, and finding a long forgotten government facility under it, with skeletons, literally in their closets, you could be sensing something that's not even there. It's pretty crazy, Katie!"

"Hey - here's something crazy! Today, just before I entered through that dungeon door, I felt something."

"I told you!"

"It was the weirdest thing I'd ever felt. I felt it again just outside the second set of swinging doors before we got to Cliff and Jon's remains."

Billie's voice was high pitched and excited. "What did you feel?"

"It felt like static electricity covering my skin. Very weird!"

"I told you I felt something down there! I felt more of a pulse - pushing us."

"You know I don't believe in ghosts and hauntings...but after today...I won't be so quick to rule it out."

"I knew you'd come around - eventually!"

"Glad I could make your night!"

"Oh - you did!" Billie giggled.

"Hey, BJ?"

"Yeah?"

"I think I should call Stella in the morning to meet us for coffee. She needs to know we found her grandfather, before the police get involved."

"I agree. I'll see you in the morning."

"Yep - have a good night."

"You too."

Katie snuggled further down into bed, disturbing Hondo's rest. He opened an eye and gave her a look. "Don't give me that look! You could be back on the floor."

Hondo gave a loud yawn, that was more of a sass back.

"I heard that!"

He stretched arching his back and straightening all four legs at once, before encroaching in on her side of the bed.

"Oh you think you're so clever." Katie gently shoved him back onto Cal's side of the bed, and then he rolled onto his back, bent paws in the air and turned back to face her.

"You're lucky you're cute!" She said with a tired smile, and snuggled with him.

In the morning Katie awoke with about 12-inches of space, Hondo had the entire bed and his hind feet in her side, with one front leg over on top of her.

Katie sighed, crawled out of bed and jumped into the shower. Hondo was still contently sleeping in her bed when she got out. "Can I interest you in some breakfast?" He opened one eye, and then the other and just stared at her. "Come on boy, let's eat!"

With that he flew off the bed and practically ran her down on the stairs. "What has gotten into you? Just because Cal is gone is no reason for you to forget your manners."

Hondo was at his food dish happily wagging his tail waiting on Katie. Normally she'd take him with her, but the past few days hadn't really given her that option. She'd have to let him out before she left and make sure to take him for a nice long walk tonight.

Katie made her sobering call to Stella. Stella was in high-spirits this morning and was happy Katie called. She wasn't sure if that was a good thing or a bad thing. News like this was very difficult to give or hear for anyone. Today Katie drove the Jeep, and parked behind the Sci-Fi Café. Billie pulled in right behind her.

"Is Stella meeting us?"

"She is, and she sounded like she was in a really good mood. I just hope when I tell her, that doesn't change too much."

"Oiy!" Billie gave Katie a grave look.

They walked in together. Brad was having a cup of coffee and reading a newspaper while listening to the weather channel on TV. In unison the girls belted out, "Good morning, Brad!"

"Hi girls!" He said with a big smile. "You've been here every day this week - I could get used to this!"

Katie answered, "Stella is meeting us for coffee; not sure if we're having breakfast yet."

"Well, speak for yourself - I want breakfast!" Billie blurted out.

Brad just laughed at their bickering.

Katie noticed they had the restaurant to themselves this morning. "Is Mary around?"

"Naw - she was up late working on her book. She's still sleepin'. You need me to wake her up?"

"No, we can fill her in later."

"You know if it's big news she won't want to be left out."

"Oh trust me - she won't be!" Katie commented as she poured herself a cup of coffee.

Billie was perusing the teas, trying to make a decision when Stella and Mary both walked in together.

"Hi girls!" Mary smiled. She did look rather tired, but she had a spark of excitement eluding from her.

Stella seemed even younger this morning. "I hope it's okay if I invited Mary to join our coffee clutch this morning - I have something thrilling to share with you all."

Billie commented, "We have a story for you, too!"

Katie flashed Billie a look.

"What? Well, we do!"

The four women sat at the tall bistro table. Stella pulled out her grandfather's brown-leather book, and a sheet of paper with a cipher on it.

"I figured it out. It's actually quite simple." Stella pointed to the line-shapes, some with dots some without. "See here."

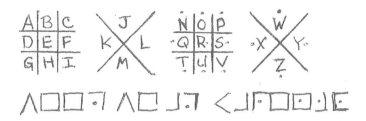

"Each one represents a letter in the grids. My Grandfather and I used to pass each other messages this way so my parents wouldn't know what we were up to. Sometimes we'd go for ice-cream, or to the five and dime for penny candy. This says - meet me at Lavern's."

Mary seemed to be vibrating out of her chair. "Tell them what you told me."

"What he wrote in this book looks like a scientific formula. He must have wanted to keep it a secret or he wouldn't have written it this way."

Katie and Billie shared a look. Katie looked back to Stella. "I think you're right about keeping it a secret. We have to tell you what we discovered after we gave that to you."

"Tell me what?"

"You said your grandfather disappeared, never to be heard from again."

"Yes."

"There's a secret government facility under that building."

Mary's eyes just about popped out of her head. "You're kidding me? This just keeps getting better!"

"Stella, we think we know what happened to your grandfather."

"What are you saying?"

"If what you have there is the formula Sadie claimed was 'too evil for anyone to have', then Jonathan Blake and Clifford Westbrook died protecting it. That book was in a wall of the 480 building, but we found two skeletons down in the sublevel at the end of the western tunnel. One we know was Cliff; I am only assuming the other one is your grandfather."

Stella's world was spinning. It was a shock after so many years, the idea that her grandfather wasn't a mobster, or a spy, but a scientist. A scientist who created something that got him killed. "Are you sure?"

"The facility held a futuristic looking lab, an office, and..." Katie hesitated, thinking about how to say it.

Billie helped Katie find the words. "A place they ran human experiments."

"What?" Mary was surprised, "And they call me a conspiracy theorist!"

Stella remained silent as she tried to wrap her head around what she was hearing. Even Brad was listening to what was going on. Luckily they were the only five people in the café.

Katie waited for Stella to say something, anything. When she didn't, Katie made a suggestion. "I'm sorry that you had to find out this way. I just wanted you to hear it from us first. Would you like us to take you down so you can see where your grandfather worked? I'd take you down before I call the police."

Stella's eyes weren't sad, they were peaceful. She gave Katie a warm smile and reached out for her hands folded in front of her. "Dear, thank you for letting me know, and for his journal. This is all I need; I don't need to visit where he worked, or where he rests now. I'd like to keep my memories of him as they are."

"Are you sure?"

"I'm sure, dear."

Mary spoke up, "Well I want to see this government facility!"

Katie chuckled, "I think we can sneak you in before we're banned from the west tunnel!"

Brad stepped in, "You ladies need to take this more seriously. Who else knows about this find?"

Katie soberly answered Brad. "The government facility or the journal?"

"Both!"

"Only the five of us here know about both. Constance and Paul Richter only know about the facility."

"Here's a piece of advice - you can take it or leave it - but my suggestion to you is that no one needs to know about that journal. If it got those men killed back in 1928 - it could be just as dangerous to have today!"

Katie and Mary both replied, "What journal?"

"As far as I'm concerned the rightful owner has it." Billie contested. "I'm not going to say anything!"

Mary looked up to her husband, "You're right, Brad, and we won't tell another soul."

*

Katie and Billie felt pretty good after telling Stella about her grandfather.

"Hey - why don't you follow me back to my place?"

Katie hopped into her Jeep as Billie led the way.

Billie unlocked the door to her apartment and was greeted by her sassy cat, Torre.

It had been a while since Katie had been to Billie Jo's. Not much had changed. Her eclectic Bohemian style fit Billie's personality completely. Katie noticed the wine bottles on top of the kitchen cabinets. "Jesus - Billie - how many bottles of Zephyr's Kiss did you take?"

Billie shrugged her shoulders. "I don't know - maybe a dozen?"

"One, two, three, four, five, six, seven, eight..." Katie began to count. "Try fifteen bottles!"

"Wow - that *is* a lot!" Billie giggled.

"You haven't tried it?"

"Nope! It's a red - I prefer something lighter and sweeter. Besides, after 85-years it's probably nasty! I just liked the bottles."

"You know, I still can't get over everything we've done. I'm happy we could give Stella and Constance some closure. It's amazing this all started because you found that diary!"

"Yeah, *and* the access to the hidden basement!"

"Yes - that's all on you, too!" Katie had to laugh. They did make a good team.

Chapter 27

Eighty-five years had passed, nevertheless murder was still murder. Knowing what she did, Katie had waited long enough to report her finding to the authorities.

Sgt. Jim Nelson was pouring a cup of coffee when Katie strolled into the sub-station. "Hey Katie!" He saw she was alone. "No Cal - must still be in D.C.?"

"Yeah..."

"What's up?"

"I need to speak with you."

"Well that doesn't sound good."

"I'm sorry, Jim; I didn't know who else to talk to about this. It's complicated."

Holding up his coffee mug, "Can I get you one?"

"Black, please."

Jim and Cal weren't just colleagues, they were good friends. He poured Katie a cup, and handed it to her before leading her down the hall to the small conference room, and shutting the door. "First - I want to know if Cal knows about whatever it is you're here for."

Katie shook her head, "No, I haven't told him yet, but I have good reason!" She sat down in one of the soft padded chairs with wheels.

Sgt. Nelsen looked to the heavens, and mumbled something under his breath. He then looked Katie in the eye, "You went back in the tunnels after you were warned not to, didn't you?"

"Not exactly."

"Oh shit - you did!" Jim sat down heavily in a chair next to Katie. "Christ - how bad is it? Wait let me guess? You found Jimmy Hoffa?"

Surprised with Jim's sarcastic reaction she just stared at him.

"Ok, just give me a number on a scale from 1-10, how bad is it?"

"That depends. What number do you give for murder?"

"Are you jerking my chain?

The expression on Katie's face told him she wasn't. "I'd definitely give murder a 10."

"Okay then, that times nine."

Sgt. Nelsen sat up, leaning across to Katie. "Times nine?"

"Billie Jo and I found 9-skeletons in an underground government facility in the west tunnel." The 'deer in the headlights' look Sgt. Nelsen was giving Katie told her she better start from the beginning.

Katie told Jim how they found the crack in the crudely blocked up entrance, and made a hole large enough for them to enter. She told him about the secret laboratory, and finally about the dungeon-like door that opened up to a section that looked like a small prison. As she revealed her story, Sgt. Nelsen scribbled notes on a yellow legal pad. He wrote so fast and so much, he periodically flipped to a clean sheet.

"Jim, this is the tricky part. The two skeletons we found in the room containing the crematorium...I know one was Cal's great-grandfather; and I'm pretty sure the other one was his partner, Jonathan Blake. By the way, if it is - he'd be Stella's grandfather."

"What makes you think that?"

"For one, I lifted Cliff's wallet and read the name on his driver's license. He also had a picture of Cal's great-grandmother, Sadie, on the inside of his hat band."

Jim gave Katie an exasperated look. "You mean to tell me Cal doesn't know any of this?"

Katie shook her head no.

"And why the hell not?"

"I did tell Cal's mother, Constance. I had to make sure what I suspected was true. When she confirmed that it was, she told me not to interrupt Cal in D.C. with this; that she would be the one to tell him."

Sgt. Nelsen rambled under his breath again. She couldn't understand what he was saying, but she did hear him say, "Cal is never going to leave you alone again."

Katie shot Jim a look and frowned. "Just so you know, I was hired to find information about that damn building! Nothing about that empty building added up. I did what anyone who wanted to find answers would have done!"

"I think we can agree, not everyone would have punched a hole in a blocked entrance!"

"Well, it's a good thing that I did, isn't it!"

Katie was incorrigible. Sgt. Nelsen just stared at her.

"Jim, just let me take you through there. I knew I had to report what I found. If you think another agency should be called then you make that call, but I think you need to see this."

"Let's go." Sgt. Nelsen moseyed to his desk, to make sure he had everything he needed. Looking across the way he spotted Officer Randy O'Brien. He stepped over to Randy's desk, "Hey, are you busy?"

"No, Sergeant."

"I need you to follow us over to the 480 building on Milwaukee."

*

Once inside the 480 building, Katie had a strange feeling something was different. She decided to chalk it up to the unpleasant history of the place. She showed them how to open the hidden passage to the basement, and led them down the narrow stone and cement stairway. O'Brien and Nelsen panned their lights around the room, observing the wine racks with some dust covered bottles of old wine.

Katie trained her light to one rack in particular, "We'll need to go through there."

The two officers followed Katie through the space behind the rack and down the tunnel to the left. Their lights soon fell upon the opening Katie and Billie made. Cautiously they followed Katie. She paused briefly at the fuse box and threw the lever, with a loud snap and humming that radiated down the tunnel. A few flickers of light, and then the soft glow of lights in tin housing buzzed to life.

Officer O'Brien was highly alert. He was making Katie more nervous than she wanted to be.

"I had no idea this was down here. I can't believe somebody hadn't found this place before now!" Sgt. Nelsen seemed to be taking it all in. It would be difficult for anyone not to get intrigued. This facility was amazing in its own right.

At the vault door, Jim stepped in using his flashlight to tear down the curtain of cobwebs.

The three stepped onto the grated platform. In the back of Jim's mind he was hoping Katie was overly exaggerating about all of this. Seeing the lab with his own two eyes, he knew she was not. What they were seeing was indescribable. According to what Katie knew to be true, this lab was functioning in the 1920's; however, it could very well have been used in the present.

"Did you want to go check it out?"

"Not unless the skeletons you found are down there?"

"No - they're further down the tunnel."

With the wave of his hand, Jim gestured for them to continue. They exited, heading west.

"That was their office." Katie mentioned as they passed.

Randy was edgy and on alert. He watched their six; every now and again he'd pause just to listen. Being down in this section of tunnel wasn't settling well with Randy.

Katie came to a stop just outside an opening. The wooden door adorned with heavy metal hardware was leaning off to one side. "This isn't how we found it. It was locked so I removed the pins from its hinges. I just really wanted to see what was behind this door." She felt the need to own up to that.

Jim and Randy's faces held a smirk, finding some humor in that.

"Through here you will find cells lining both sides of the tunnel, with seven skeletons. Once we get through to the end there will be a set of swinging doors. There is more light passed those doors."

Jim entered first leading the way, Katie and then Randy following behind. Everything Katie had told Jim was true. No embellishment was needed; this was just as surreal as she had said it would be.

They shinned their lights in each and every cell along the way. The dark recesses played tricks with their sight. Every time light entered that space the dark shadow phantoms spirited away only to return as soon as the light left again.

"This is fucked up!" Jim commented.

Randy was fairly quiet. It was an unbelievable sight to see. Just before passing through the swinging double doors at the end, he paused. Randy felt something. Sensed something. Whatever it was, it made him uneasy.

Jim was already inspecting the medical tools on the cart. "You think they were doing some kind of experiments on those guys out there?"

"That's what it looks like. I figure once you do the forensics we'll know more."

Randy came in and saw Jim holding a very large syringe with a trigger. "Jesus - Nelsen, put that down!

You might hurt someone." He was teasing, but the tools on that cart were enough to scare even the bravest man.

They had a good laugh; it was brief, but it broke some of the tension.

Katie then pointed to the second set of swinging doors. "The skeletons of the two scientists are through there."

Jim asked, "What's in there?"

"A crematorium", she answered.

Sgt. Nelsen and Officer O'Brien shared a look. Jim slowly opened one of the doors. Stepping in he and O'Brien scanned the room. At the far end of the room was a crematorium. There were wooden crates stacked up on one side. A laundry cart bulging with abandoned clothing, and a glass jar containing what looked like human teeth with gold fillings, sat on a desk. Between them and the desk were the skeletal remains of two individuals.

Katie commented, "The one with the hat is Cal's great-grandfather. I looked inside his wallet and the New York driver's license said Clifford Westbrook. I can only assume the other one is Stella's grandfather, Jonathan Blake. He was Cliff's partner."

Randy gave Katie a strange look. She recognized it as a "cop" look. They all have that one certain look when they want answers. She obliged without having to be asked, "I know because Constance told me some of their family history, as well as reading Sadie's diary. She was Cliff's wife. I found an old photo of Sadie inside the hat band. I gave it to Constance."

The frown Randy gave her, told her she shouldn't have taken anything, but she wasn't going to let it bother her.

Sgt. Nelsen blew out a breath. "Well, let's get the M.E. down here. We're going to treat it as a crime scene." He placed a hand on Katie's shoulder. "How long ago did you say this was?"

"Eighty-five years."

"How do you know that?"

"The last entry date in Sadie's diary was from 1928, the same time as Stella's grandfather disappeared."

Jim raised a brow, "Mitch is going to love this one!"

They trekked back through the tunnel, into the basement and up the narrow stairs leading into the 480 building, just as Paul was coming back down the stairs from the 3rd floor. The awkwardness was felt by all four.

"Paul! I didn't know you were going to be here today."

Paul looked to Sgt. Nelsen and then to Officer O'Brien standing behind Katie. "I didn't realize you were giving tours."

Katie furrowed her brow. It was a strange comment. One she didn't expect coming from Paul. "I just reported the remains I found. Constance knows."

Paul smiled, but the look in his eyes was odd. "Sergeant, is there anything you will need from us?"

Sgt. Nelsen eyed Paul. He felt Katie's suspicion of Paul Richter without her having to say a word. "Not at this time. We'll let you know."

"Well, I'll let you get to it then."

"Paul, anything I could help you with?"

Paul looked to Sgt. Nelsen and Officer O'Brien, and then back to Katie. "That's okay, just had to check on a few things for myself."

Chapter 28

After the interesting call the medical examiner, Mitch Carter received, he packed what he needed and headed over to the 480 building. He couldn't wait to see why it was to be hush-hush. This was relatively a small town, with small town gossip. Anytime a fire truck, ambulance or squad car showed up anywhere - it was an attraction. Showing up with the M.E. van was like national news!

Officer Randy O'Brien and Sgt. Nelsen stayed behind down in the west tunnel with the skeletal remains, while Billie and Katie waited for Mitch. This was a unique situation. One that Sgt. Nelsen allowed Katie and Billie to escort the M.E. down to them. He pulled around and parked in the back. The 9-body bags were folded and stuffed in a tack pack, which he carried with him.

Mitch smiled at the sight of Billie and Katie. "Jack and Cal can't leave you two to your own devises!" He chuckled. "Come on - show me what you found now!"

The girls secretly dreaded Jack and Cal's return, knowing they would never hear the end of this one!

Locking the door to the 480 building so inquiring busy bodies couldn't walk in on what was happening. Billie even pulled the shade on the door for good measure. They led Mitch down the narrow stone and concrete steps into the basement and through the tunnel to the west.

Sgt. Nelsen and Randy O'Brien had set up lights all the way down the tunnel. There wasn't any need for carrying flashlights now.

Mitch followed the girls. "Hold up!"

The girls stopped and turned back. Mitch was standing at the opened vault door peering inside.

"What is this place?"

"We believe it's a government facility, one I imagine they never thought we'd find." Katie answered.

He stepped out onto the grated platform looking down into the impressive lab. "This is truly amazing." He admired what he saw from where they stood. "Girls, I know this isn't the time, but one of these days, I'd love to hear how you found all this."

Billie giggled, "Maybe we could tell Jack and Cal at the same time...then they won't be so mad about it."

That made Mitch smile; he knew his son.

They continued on passed the office. Mitch took a quick peek inside. The girls stopped and waited for Mitch to catch up to them. Before long, they came to the entrance where the dungeon-like door hung. Nelsen and O'Brien now had it lit up like an operating room, very bright. The dark creepy tomb-like space didn't have the same feel anymore. This time looking inside each cell seemed more like a museum than doom and gloom.

First Mitch took his time looking in each cell all the way down. He counted seven sets of remains. He asked Sgt. Nelsen, "Where are the other two?"

Jim held open a swinging door. "Through there", he said pointing to the next set of doors.

Katie and Billie walked with him so they could tell him what they knew about the last two. After the girls told Mitch about Sadie's diary, and the connection to Stella and Cal, he understood why the secrecy. "I will take great care of them." He reassured Katie and Billie.

It wasn't just the historical aspect of this find that was thrilling for Mitch, but also the connection. However, there was an even more disturbing and darker thought he had about this. Anyone could see this was part of some government operation. Whoever killed these men, and buried this facility to keep its secrets wouldn't want it to be found.

Mitch took his time with the help from Randy, to bag each set of remains. He took photos before he did, and made notes so he could tell them apart, for his own piece of mind. When all seven were removed from their cells, he moved onto the last two.

The skeleton only makes up about 15% of their body weight. Since all nine are skeletal remains, each bag of bones weighs approximately 20-30 pounds. They stacked them and carried them out in teams of two.

Mitch wanted to get them in his morgue and lock them up away from prying eyes right away.

*

The morgue wasn't very large. It was only a 20' X 25' room, not including the large walk-in cooler on one side. On a busy day he could have up to four bodies in there, and that has only happed twice in his career. Now he was looking around the room filled with nine bodies, laying side-by-side, some on borrowed gurneys. "Where do I begin?" He said aloud to himself. No one heard him; aside from the nine sets of remains zipped up in black bags around the room, he was alone.

He decided to start taking samples of bone and teeth, from the ones with visible skeletal and dental fluorosis. Then he took his time with the remains of Clifford Westbrook and who they believe to be Jonathan Blake. It would take him possibly a week to examine them all.

When examining the remains of Clifford Westbrook, the first thing Mitch found a Patek Philippe wrist watch. It was a beautiful piece. He'd make sure the Chapman's got that back. After removing what was left of the tattered clothes, he found a spent .38 round. Upon further examination, he discovered a nick in a rib where the bullet had entered. Speculating, this is what killed Cliff.

When Mitch was finished with Cliff's remains, he moved on to Jonathan Blake's. He also found a spent .38 round with his remains. He couldn't find any cracks or nicks in the bones, which lead him to believe his was a soft tissue entrance, probably a gut shot.

It was time to call it a day. After many hours of examining, note taking, and taking more photos, Mitch was tired; but he felt good about his work. After getting home he took a long shower thinking about the girls' discovery and what it could mean not only to the families involved but also the community. He put three cubes of ice in a rocks glass and poured three fingers of Glenfiddich. He sat back in his recliner, turning to the news channel on TV, just for some background noise. Looking down into his glass, Mitch swirled the cubes of ice in the golden liquor. He took a pull, enjoying the taste and the warmth of the scotch.

He picked the receiver off its cradle and called his son. He knew Jack would be home in a day or two, but felt he better give him a heads up before he came home.

It rang a few times and went to voice mail. "Jack - its Dad. Call me when you get this." He hung up, and the phone instantly rang back.

"Dad - is everything alright?"

The smile on Mitch's face grew wide. "Everything is just fine, Jack. However, I felt you should have fair warning..."

"Warning about what?"

"You'll never guess what Katie and your girlfriend have been up to!"

Jack was speechless for a moment or two. He looked to TJ and Midas sitting across the fire pit from him. He let out a heavy sigh, "What did they do now?"

Mitch sipped his scotch as he filled his son in on what was happening back home. Although their conversation was mostly one-sided, the tone in Jack's voice told him they were cutting their fishing trip short. "You don't need to come home early. That's not why I called! I just didn't want this to be a surprise to you when you returned."

There was a long pause on the line.

Mitch finally spoke, "I'll see you when you get here."

TJ noticed Jack's apprehension. "What's up?"

Jack shook his head with frustration, "BJ and Katie went right back down into the tunnels as soon as we left town!"

TJ laughed. The humor wasn't lost on him; after all it was the girls who discovered where the bikers hid the stolen military weapons and their Meth lab to give them the break they needed for their RICO case against the 7-Sons of Sin.

"They discovered an abandoned government lab with a few sets of remains!" Jack glared at TJ. "No joke!"

The sudden look of concern on Midas' face told Jack, he already knew about the hidden underground lab.

Other Titles by

Tammy Teigland

A Stranger in the Night

Taken

7 Sons of Sin

Coming Soon: *Deception*

To Contact Tammy Teigland, or to be placed on a mailing list to receive updates about new releases, visit her website:

www.tammyteigland.com

A new series from A Stranger in the Night.

Deception

Cal thought he had left D.C. behind for good, but after the short flight from Milwaukee, Wisconsin, here he was, right back where he left off nearly 10-years ago. Thinking back as he made his way to baggage claim, a woman stepped out of the ladies' room and right into Cal. "Oh - pardon, me."

The intriguingly beautiful woman with long sable colored hair looked at him with surprise and smiled. With that, she turned and vanished into the crowd.

Now that he was back in Washington, he needed to amp up his awareness level and watch his six. Cal still did not know who broke into his home, or what they wanted. Walking through the airport with blinders on was not good he told himself. He shook the fog from his mind and snatched his bag from the luggage carousel, before heading for the exit.

As Cal passed through the terminal doors, Mason pulled up to the curb in his '67 Chevy Biscayne.

Mason had timed his pick-up perfectly.

Cal smiled with fond memories at the sight of Mason in his old car.

Mason hopped out of the car to open the trunk. "Howdy, stranger!"

Cal just shook his head in disbelief. "You still have this old rat?"

"Be kind to her my friend, she is your ride." He said with a slight Okie dialect. "How the hell have ya'll been?" Mason welcomed Cal, extending his right hand and brought him in with a half hug. "I missed you, man. You know, the Bureau isn't the same without ch'ya." Mason joked.

Cal chuckled, "After 10 years in D.C. you still have that southern drawl... is that real or just for the ladies?"

Mason raised a brow, feeling almost insulted, but then winked as he blew Cal a kiss.

An irritated horn blew behind them.

"Yeah, yeah - don't get your panties in a bunch!" Mason grumbled.

They climbed into the dark Chevy. With the turn of a key Mason started her up with a loud rumble, and headed out onto George Washington Parkway.

It was Mason who introduced Cal to old muscle cars. The 1967 Biscayne was Mason's father's car. A roughneck from Oklahoma who had been killed in a job-related accident. He did not have much, but what he did have, he left to Mason. Cal noticed the car looked the same, but now instead of sounding like she was choking on her last breath, she ran and sounded, like one mean machine. "I can tell you've been working on her."

"Yeah, well... I found I had lots of extra time and money once Chrissie left."

"Hey man, I'm sorry to hear that."

Mason snapped, "Me too! The bitch even took my dog! Who does that? That's just plain mean." After a long pause, "I really miss that dog!"

Cal sympathetically smiled, and shook his head. He did not realize how much he missed his old partner. Glancing out the window passed Mason toward the Pentagon, Cal wondered.

Mason caught his glance, "He knows you're in town."

"That doesn't surprise me. My ol' man always seems to know everything."

"Actually, I told him." Giving Cal a sideways glance, "*And* we're having dinner with him tomorrow night."

Cal raised a curious brow to Mason.

"By the way he's glad you're here."

Cal turned his head to the right staring out his side window in silence.

Stillness filled the car as they crossed the Potomac. Soon they drove up to the J. Edgar Hoover Building, a massive beige concrete building heavily embellished with cameras; seen and unseen eyes everywhere. FBI cars, trucks and unmarked white vans lined 10th Street. A K-9 unit drove past them turning onto Pennsylvania Ave. Secretly Cal wondered if there was anyone left that he would remember. He knew Stacey had moved on and was now working for CID (Criminal Investigation Department). Grateful there was no threat of running into his old girlfriend anytime soon. For Cal, coming back here was awkward enough. Deep down, he felt like a failure. Cal would not be able to forgive himself for walking away if they find the killer to be the same man who murdered the first escort. Ten years ago, he was so cock sure it had been the Russian diplomat's son. He now had his doubts; what if it was not? He hated the way the State Department handled things, subsequently like a spoiled child he picked up his ball and left. Politics aside, he should have stayed. He should have stuck it out; however, there was no time for 'what if's'.

Pulling under the monolithic building, with its square bronzed windows scrutinizing their every move, Mason parked the old Chevy. "I've got to get you checked in. Davidson has vouched for you and has agreed to give you the same access as me."

Surprised, "Robert Davidson? How did you manage that?"

"Actually, it was *his* idea. He said at the time he thought you were too close to this." Mason followed it up with, "But he's always respected you."

"Why are you stroking my ego, Stone?"

With a crooked grin, "Because we're gonna to see Davidson, first."

"Gee, thanks for the heads up!"

They made their way up to Davidson's office. A few female agents turned their heads to eye the handsome men passing through; however, most of the agents they passed along the way did not pay Cal much attention, it was Stone they eyed.

Agent Stone knocked on the director's door.

"Enter!" Was the command that came from behind the closed door.

Cal followed Mason in and closed the door behind them.

Director Robert Davidson was seated behind his impressive dark walnut desk. Neatly groomed, and wearing a designer suit. His grey piercing eyes and cold chiseled expression set the tone. He stood, extending a hand in Cal's direction, "Detective Chapman…" the men exchanged confident glances, "We're glad to have your assistance on this."

Cal returned the handshake, "Thank you, Sir."

"Please - take a seat."

Cal noticed the office smelled of leather and books.

Davidson did not beat around the bush. "Ten years ago, you left us because of the way things were handled with the State Department."

Cal shifted uneasily in his chair, like a kid having to face the school principal.

"I get it. I really do, Chapman. But - you were wrong."

"Sir?"

"I believe you were on the right track… except back then, someone screwed the pooch; which led you down not necessarily the wrong path, but a parallel one."

Cal furrowed his brow.

"On your exit you said something that made me take another look. Dmitri, we knew was involved… but he did not kill her. I smelled a cover-up."

"How do I fit into this?"

"Hey, this was your case. You lived it, breathed it, woke up with it and slept on it every night. Agent Stone will give you everything we have on this new case. I need you to take a look. *You* tell *me* if we're looking at the same killer."

Cal gave Director Davidson a considerate nod.

Opening a desk drawer, the director reached in to retrieve an envelope and tossed it across his desk to Cal. "These are for you." Cal stared blankly as a manila folder that held the contents of so many hours of his life, slid to an abrupt halt, directly in front of him.

"You will be our consultant on this case, but I want you to understand that you will be more than just a consultant... I am granting you the same access as Agent Stone. Consider yourselves partners, again."

Sounding more surprised than he wanted to, "Thank you, Sir." Cal reached down for the folder as he shook the director's hand.

"Don't thank me yet!" The director gave Cal a solemn nod. "This is a 'hot topic' here on the political landscape of D.C. and heavily scrutinized from upstairs."

Considering the director's last comment with a slight cock of his head, he followed Mason out of the office. Once outside he turned to his newly reacquired partner. "Did you receive my packages?"

"Yep!"

"We should probably get started." Cal held the door open and motioned forward without missing a beat as Mason passed by him on the way through the doorway.

"Agreed." He paused and waited for Cal to catch up, "Looks like we're going to Georgetown!" He carried that familiar grin of determination and persistence. "I don't know about you, but I need some lunch."

"Georgetown?" There was a tone of surprise in Cal's voice, "Nick's is still open?"

"You remembered?" Mason chuckled.

Cal laughed in obligatory response, "Of course, I remember Nick's Riverside Grill."

***

Finding a quiet booth facing the door, the two old friends ordered lunch.

"Sooo..." Cal stretched out his inquiry, with less of a sour annotation than he remembered having. "What makes you and Davidson believe me *now,* about a cover-up?"

Mason focused on his beer while he went back over the facts in his head. "We know Dmitri was trafficking women and still is. Sex trafficking is a huge business. There is lots of money to be made." He nodded towards Cal as he spoke, "Your dead escort was one of Dmitri's. However, we now believe he was angry about her *death - not* that we arrested him for it." Mason took a sip of beer as he waited for Cal to take that all in and signaled toward Cal as he set it back down. "Dmitri was quiet, because there is more to it. Think about it."

"Say that is true..." Cal leaned toward Mason, lowering his head across the table, "Who would scare a kid connected to the Russian mob, enough to keep him quiet?"

A smirk tugged at Mason's lips, "Who says he was scared?" Mason lifted his drink from its coaster as Cal inched back into his seat from across the table, a cold beer hovered just below Mason's mouth as he continued, "It's not like we threatened him with a Turkish prison or Gitmo..." Mason's drink met his lips as he finished, "Our prison system is like booking a room at the Hyatt for these guys. We didn't do jack, except slow down whatever he was already up to."

Cal took a swig from his bottle as Mason continued.

"You and I had three persons of interest, but only two still stand out in my mind; Dmitri, and we both know how *that one* worked out, and Senator Devin Voss."

Setting his bottle down, Cal responded, *"Senator?"*

Mason sat up, and leaned in, "Well, he wasn't a Senator then!"

Cal shot Mason a look. "Tell me about this last girl." He fidgeted with the edge of his coaster as he set down his near empty beer.

The waitress brought their food, interrupting their conversation and asked if they needed another round while she was there. Cal lifted his bottle toward her and she nodded as she walked away, both remaining silent until they were certain she was out of 'ear shot' of the table.

Mason reached for the pickle on his plate and took a large bite as he continued. "The escort was young and beautiful; I mean *model* beautiful..." He waved his half-eaten pickle in Cal's direction and reached for a fry as he explained, "Not a blemish on her. She was well groomed and manicured." He spoke with his mouth full, covering a fry and waving it around like a maestro, emphasizing key points tipped in ketchup. "The most interesting thing about her... our medical examiner found a microchip embedded in the back of her neck at the hairline." He stopped chewing long enough to come up for air and take a swig of beer.

Cal narrowed his eyes, glaring down and examining his meal, "Odd."

"Oh" Mason jabbed another fry Cal's way, "It gets better!"

Intently listening to Mason's summations as he evaluated where to begin on his plate, Cal tried to get a feeling for this case. "Tell me again how she was found."

"That's the eerie part." Mason paused. "She was displayed just like the one 10-years ago." He looked around the room from side to side, like a nervous Mob boss as he continued, "I don't know what you think about it, but I have a feeling she's a message for somebody."

"How so?" Cal cocked his head a bit.

Mason wiped his hands on his napkin and leaned towards Cal with both hands. "There's the location of the dump, the artful way in which both bodies were displayed and both were high-end escorts with connections to prominent political players. But this one…" Mason leaned back in his chair and threw the napkin at the side of his plate for emphasis, "*This one* - I want to say - was a little *too* perfectly posed."

"Like a set-up?"

"I think so!" Mason dropped his arms to his side and leaned back in.

"Mase," Cal referring to him so casually while they talked about work, was unusual for Cal, "Tell me about the location of the dump."

Mason pulled out a photograph from the expand-file he brought in with him. He set it on the table, just to the right of Cal.

"It's the same location?" Cal looked up from his furrowed eyebrows.

"Yep!" Mason did not move a muscle.

Cal studied the photo for several seconds. His mind flashed back to the original murder 10-years ago.

"What?" Mason was silently studying Cal's face. "Do you see something?"

Cal just shook his head no. "Just remembering back is all."

"If you want – we can head over to the site after lunch." Cal threw down the napkin on his now empty plate and leaned back in the chair as a man after meal, often does. "I mean some time has passed, but who knows, you might see something they missed?"

Mason stretched his arms behind his head with confidence, "What I *do* know, is that the autopsy revealed the same two marks left by a stun gun and her teeth were slightly fractured. I want to say damage from the high voltage on the stun gun." Mason dropped his arms to his sides and inched forward. "Whoever did this –" His voice lowered and softened as he spoke. "Incapacitated her before killing her - in the same manner as the last one." He lowered his head before leveling back up to Cal's face, eye to eye now, "My guess - is they didn't know, *this one* was chipped, though."

Cal remained focused. "Have they been able to track where this chip came from?"

"We sent it out," Mason eased off, "Hope to hear soon."

Cal chewed on that, and filed that information away for later. "Tell me about Dmitri Medvedev."

"You'll *love* this..." His arms widened to their fullest capacity and he reeled them back in to position, "He's back in the States and is now using the alias Dmitri Mogilevich. Not very creative, I know, but I have been keeping an eye on him. He's been rubbing elbows with high society as an art dealer."

"An art dealer?"

"It's legit, too! He has a gallery in the warehouse district and he owns the property!"

"Does the State Department know?"

"Let's just say we're *all* keeping close tabs on him."

"Who's he been getting cozy with?"

Mason sat back, taking a long pull from his beer. A smile spread across his face. "Juliette Voss."

Cal sat forward. "Any relation to Senator Voss?" He asked quietly.

"Yep! His wife!"

Made in the USA
Monee, IL
18 March 2024

55137597R00134